W9-CEN-558

WRONG PLACE. WRONG TIME.

"Are you ready?" cried Silvertip. "Then fill your hand!"

The form whirled toward him, the cloak fanning well out to the side. One hand rose, as if to let go with the gun it seemed to hold. The other did not rise.

"Take it then, damn you!" muttered Silvertip, and drawing, he fired.

The finger of red fire flicked out of the muzzle of the gun, as though pointing the way for the bullet with the death it carried. That flash showed Silvertip not the face of Bandini, but a dark-skinned handsome youth. The horror in those wide eyes flashed at Silvertip for an instant and then the inflooding darkness covered the falling body.

Silvertip could not move; he could not catch the weight before it struck solidly against the ground. The dust that puffed out under the impact rose in a cloud, acrid against the nostrils of Silvertip.

A SILVERTIP ADVENTURE

MAX BRAND

SILVERTIP

BERKLEY BOOKS, NEW YORK

The characters, places, incidents and situations in this book are imaginary and have no relation to any person, place or actual happening.

This Berkley book contains the complete
text of the original hardcover edition.

SILVERTIP

A Berkley Book / published by arrangement with
G. P. Putnam's Sons

PRINTING HISTORY
Warner edition / October 1973
Berkley edition / November 1989

All rights reserved.
Copyright 1933 by Frederick Faust.
Copyright renewed 1961 by Jane F. Easton, Miss Judith Faust,
and Mr. John Frederick Faust.
This book may not be reproduced in whole or in part,
by mimeograph or any other means, without permission.
For information address: G. P. Putnam's Sons,
200 Madison Avenue, New York, New York 10016.

ISBN: 0-425-11840-1

A BERKLEY BOOK ® TM 757,375
Berkley Books are published by The Berkley Publishing Group,
200 Madison Avenue, New York, New York 10016.
The name "Berkley" and the "B" logo
are trademarks belonging to Berkley Publishing Corporation.

PRINTED IN THE UNITED STATES OF AMERICA

10 9 8 7 6 5 4 3 2 1

CHAPTER I

Beckoning Lights

"SILVERTIP" was what men called him, since the other names he chose to wear were as shifting as the sands of the desert; but he was more like a great stag than a grizzly. For he was built heavy to the waist; below, he was as slender as any swift-running deer. Yet the nickname was no accident. Above his young face, high up in the hair over his temples, appeared two tufts of gray that at times and in certain lights had the look of small horns. For this reason the Mexicans were apt to call him "El Diablo," but Americans knew him as Silvertip, which they shortened often to Silver, or Tip.

On this day, he had ridden out of the green of the higher mountains, and now, among the brown foothills, he sat on his mustang and looked over the gray of the arid plains below. The day had hardly stopped flushing the upper peaks with color, but night was already rolling in across the plain beneath. It covered the river; it covered Cruces for a few moments, also, but then the lights of the town began to shine through.

The place glimmered in the thickening welter of shadows, and as Silvertip watched the gleaming, he remembered the little garden restaurant of Antonio Martinelli, down yonder in Cruces. He remembered the taste of the acrid red wine, and the heaping plates of spaghetti, seasoned with Bolognese sauce and powdered with Parmesan cheese.

He knew, then, why he had ridden down through the upper valleys. It was not only because the law did not threaten him, at the moment, but because he was a little tired of venison or mountain grouse roasted over a camp fire. It was dangerous for him to leave the fastnesses and descend into the plains, for even when the law did not want him, there were always sundry men who did. If they could not pull him down single-handed, they would try in numbers. They had tried before, and his body was streaked and spotted with silver where their grip had touched him.

But just as an old grizzly rouses from the winter sleep in the highlands and looks off the brow of some mountain promontory down into the shadows of the plains, remembering the danger of guns and dogs and men, feeling his ancient wounds ache, but recalling also the taste of fat beef and, above all, the delight of the dangerous game—so Silvertip looked down into the shadows and smiled a little. With an unconscious reaction, his right hand went up under his coat to the butt of the six-gun that hung beneath the pit of his left arm, in a clip holster; then Silver started the gelding down into the night.

It was not long before his horse was slipping and stumbling over the water-polished rocks at the bottom of the ford; then the close warmth within the streets of the town received him, the half-sweet, half-pungent odors. The children were still playing, flashing through pale shafts of lamplight and turning dim in the darkness beyond; the house dogs ran with them; only the pigs had gone to sleep.

A sense of comfortable security began to come over Silvertip. He fought against that as a traveler in the arctic struggles against the fatal drowsiness of cold. He sat straighter in the saddle, shrugged back his shoulders, expanded his nostrils to take a deeper breath. As he rode on, his head automatically kept turning a trifle from side to side while his practiced eyes, with side glances, studied the houses at hand and all the street behind him, as well as the way before.

He had to go most of the way through Cruces before he came to the jingling sound of a mandolin and the noise of jolly laughter that told him he was near Antonio Martinelli's place. It stood off by itself, surrounded by the olive trees and grapevines, which only the pain of Italian handwork could make flourish in the dry West. The two windmills which gave life and greenness to that spot were both whirling their wheels high overhead with a soft, well-oiled clanking.

He did not go directly in, but first rode past the lighted front of the saloon, hotel, and restaurant; for Martinelli's place was complete. He rode close, piercing the windows with his glance, peering over the top of the swinging doors of the saloon through the smoke wreaths at the faces within. All seemed friendliness and cheer; the dangerous feeling of security welled up in him, again, irresistibly. His taut mind relaxed as a body relaxes, after labor, in a warm bath.

He rode straight back around the building to the stable, and led the mustang inside. The horse drew back, cowering a little. It snorted and stamped; it trembled at the unfamiliarness of inclosing walls, for it was as wild as the mountains among which Silvertip had caught it.

High up on the mow, a voice was singing. Hay rustled and thumped down into a manger.

"Hey, Piero!" called Silvertip.

"Hey? Who's there?" called the voice of a man from the top of the haymow. Then, as though the tones of Silvertip had gradually soaked deeper into his memory: "Oh, Silver! Is it Silvertip?"

"Yes," said Silver.

"I am coming—quickly!" panted Piero Martinelli. "Oh, Silver, this is good! Is it safe for you to be here? Are we to hide you? Must I talk softly? How long will you stay? Father will be happy—mother will dance and sing. Ah, Silvertip," he finished, as he came breathless to the bottom of the ladder and gripped the hand of the larger man, "how happy I am to see you again!"

"I knew your singing, and I knew your song, Piero,"

7

said Silver. "And I don't have to hide, this time. Look out —this is a wild devil of a horse."

"I know," said Piero, laughing. "You don't like tame things; you like them wild. Oh, we all know about that. I won't come near those heels. Does it bite and strike?"

"Like a mountain lion," said Silvertip, stripping the saddle from the round, strong barrel of the horse. "There's plenty of hay for him. Will you come in with me? Are you through here?"

"Of course I'm through," said Piero. "The work ends when you come. I'll tell every one that—"

"No," cautioned Silvertip. "Don't do that. I want a corner table in the garden; to be as quiet as possible; to hear the singing; to eat pounds of spaghetti. You know, Piero, that the day has passed when I could walk into a crowd and be comfortable. It's bad medicine for me to have any one standing at my back."

"Ah, ah," groaned the other. "I know! Well, we'll go in the side door."

They walked out into the open, following a curving path covered with gravel. The step of Piero was a loud crunching, but the foot of Silver, in spite of his weight, made hardly a sound.

"Tell me who's inside," said Silvertip.

"All good fellows," answered Piero. "All except one."

"Never mind about the others, then. Tell me about him."

"The Mexican, Bandini, he—"

"You mean José Bandini?"

"Yes, that one—with the record of killing so many men—that same José Bandini."

"He's a bad hombre," remarked Silvertip, pausing. "And there's an old grudge between us."

"Hi!" exclaimed Piero under his breath. "Is there an old grudge? And will he face you? Will he really dare to face *you*, Silver?"

"He'll face anybody if he has to," answered Silver. "But he'd rather shoot from behind. Bandini's there, is he? Well, that's bad." He walked on, slowly, saying in addition: "I know him and I know his record. But his killings are mostly talk. Like mine, Piero. You know what they say of me, and it's mostly talk."

"Ah—yes?" murmured Piero politely. Then he went

on, with a touch of passion: "That Bandini is with another Mexican—a young man—a very fine-looking young Mexican. They are eating together in one of the small rooms. Bandini is making trouble. We hear their voices jump up high, for a minute or two, and then drop away, again. There is a lot of trouble between them. My mother is worried."

"If Bandini's talking," said Silvertip, "you don't need to worry. That sort of snake doesn't rattle before it strikes."

They went in through a side door into a kitchen filled with smoke and whirling wreaths of steam, for all the cooking was done at a great open hearth, with black pots hoisted on cranes in various places above the flames. Two women were working, one slender and young, one overflowing with fat and energy and high spirits. Her rosy face grew redder still when she saw Silvertip. She threw out her arms as though she would embrace him, and then with moist hands, took both of his and struck them softly together.

"Ah, Silver," she cried, "I speak of you, and you come. But I am always speaking of you, and you are seldom here. Look, Maria! Do you see him? He is bigger than I said, eh? See the gray spots in his hair? See how brown he is, too, and how his eyes laugh. See how he smiles, exactly as I said; mostly with his eyes. Look at him! You'll never see such a man again, so good and so bad and so gentle and cruel and so much of everything that we love. We have reason to love him; I've told you the reason, too."

The girl began to blush and laugh. Silvertip, with that faint smile of his, picked a handful of smoke out of the air and made as though to throw it into the face of Mrs. Martinelli.

"What do you have, Silver?" she asked him. "Antonio has a bottle of red wine saved for you. It is the last of the old wine, that you liked. It is down in the cellar, covered with dust, old with waiting for you. But what will you eat? Look—here are Spanish beans—yonder is roast kid —here's roast chicken. Look at the brown of it, Silver! And here—"

"Spaghetti, that's what I want," said Silvertip.

"Spaghetti of course, and then?"

"Spaghetti first, with that meat sauce, and lots of Parmesan cheese to sprinkle on it. I can't think about what I'll want next until I've looked at that spaghetti."

"You see, Maria?" said Mrs. Martinelli. "I told you that he was true Italian. He will have his *pasta*. And if—"

"No!" cried a voice from beyond the wall on the left. "No, José!"

That cry struck a silence through the kitchen, and banished all the smiles except that quiet smile of Silvertip which was so often on his face.

"There! There!" whispered Mrs. Martinelli. "You hear, Silver? It's Bandini. There's murder in the air. It's Bandini—and he means to kill, I'm sure."

"Tush," said Silver. "He's talking too much. There'll be no shooting."

"Ah," said Mrs. Martinelli, "you may say that, but I tell you, Silver, that a man's eyes—even your eye—can only see what it falls on. But I see something more. And there is death in the air to-night. Some one will die before the kind daylight comes back."

A door opened, with a sudden bang, and José Bandini stood on the kitchen threshold.

CHAPTER II

The Shot in the Dark

EVEN without the force of his reputation, Bandini would have given pause to the eye and the mind of any observer. He was one of those tall men with narrow shoulders and long fingers, who are strong as apes in spite of their slenderness. Of the meager width of his shoulders he was very conscious, and usually wore, as he was doing now, a cloak with a wide-flaring collar. He was dressed like a Mexican cow-puncher on holiday, with a silk shirt and a colorful scarf tied about his hips. But nothing mattered, on second glance, except the face of the man. For it was built back from the chin in a series of steps, all rugged. Chin and mouth, nose, brow, receded in due order, and yet there was plenty of brain capacity in that head. It was a handsome face, in a strange way, time-battered, life-worn; and at will Bandini could be either charmingly pleasant, or savagely dangerous.

He was dangerous now. He thrust forward his head a little and blazed his eyes at Mrs. Martinelli.

"You woodenhead!" he shouted. "Where's the pepper sauce for those frijoles? And send me a waiter with another face, because if I see the fool again, I'm going to scramble his brains on the floor!"

Suddenly he was silent. He had seen the face of Silvertip, and the faint, small smile on it. The fingers of the right hand of Bandini made a sudden movement which could hardly be followed; it was the sign against the evil eye. The glance of Bandini lifted to the small gray tufts, like incipient horns, high above the temples of Silvertip.

"Señor Silver," said Bandini, and made an ironic bow. Then he came across the room, deliberately. It was plain that he was afraid, but a devil of the perverse in him forced him on into the danger. He stood right in front of Silvertip, and eye to eye.

"Have you come to see me, señor?" he asked.

Silvertip said nothing. He kept on smiling, and looking. The moment lasted ten grim seconds. Suddenly Bandini turned white, and shouted:

"Have you come here to insult me? You know where to find me! Bandini does not run!"

"I want to talk with you," said Silver. "Come outside into the dark for a moment, will you?"

Bandini turned yellow-white about the corners of his mouth.

"Only for talking; I want a word with you alone," said Silver.

"Dark or light and day or night, I avoid no man," said Bandini, and went out through the door with a swagger that brushed his cloak against both sides of it.

Silver took heed of the round eyes of fear that were fixed upon him from both sides, and he reassured them with a smile. Then he stepped behind Bandini into the darkness, and pulled the door shut behind him.

There was only starlight here, and the stars were dim lanterns by which to follow the movements of a Bandini. Silver became just a trifle more alert than a hunting cat.

"Now!" breathed Bandini. "And what do you want?"

"I want some news," said Silver. "I want to know about the fellow who's having dinner with you. I want to know what's in the air."

"Just a fool of a boy—that's all he is," said Bandini, after a moment. But there was that in his eyes that made Silvertip yearn to see the face. A single glint of light would have helped then, to reveal a story. "And what business is it of yours?"

"It ought to be every man's business," said Silvertip, "to watch you. No good ever came out of you, Bandini."

"Do you insult me?" snarled the Mexican.

"You don't understand me, Bandini," said Silvertip. "I don't insult you. A man doesn't insult a rattlesnake; he shoots it. And that's what will happen between us, before the wind-up."

He heard no answer—only the heavy, irregular breathing of the Mexican. Bandini was afraid—sick with fear—and Silver knew it.

"Every man who has ever seen you at work has reasons enough to wish you dead, Bandini. That's why I'm asking you what deviltry you're up to with that other young Mexican, to-night?"

No matter what fear there was in Bandini, he exclaimed suddenly: "Is every man to tell you his secrets—or be murdered?"

Silver, gritting his teeth slowly together, mused on that answer before he said: "I've seen you deal crooked cards; I've seen the scar of your knife left on a man's *back;* I knew some of the dead men you've left behind you. Now you're at some deviltry again, and you're not going through with it, if I can help it. I'm going to give you time to think it over. Pull yourself together and make up your mind.

"There's no reason why we should spoil our dinners about this. But by nine thirty I'll look for you in front of the restaurant—anywhere on the street in front of it. If you're there, I'll know that you want to have it out with me. If you're not there, I'll know that you've left town. But if you're neither in the street nor out of town, I'm going to start looking for you, Bandini, and I'll break down doors until I get at you. It was never intended that rats like you should go about the world gnawing at the lives of honest men!"

There was another moment of pause; he heard, again, the hurried breathing of the Mexican, like that of a man who has been running hard. Then Bandini turned on his heel. His cloak swished with a whispering sound through the air, and he passed back into the kitchen. As Silvertip entered in turn, the farther door banged behind Bandini,

13

and Silver stepped into a strained moment of silence in the kitchen.

Silver turned with a sudden cheerfulness to Piero.

"If there's a corner table in the garden, I'm going to have it, Piero."

"Come!" said Piero Martinelli.

"No," said Silvertip. "Quietly does the trick. I'll find my way. I'm hungry for that spaghetti, Mrs. Martinelli."

Then he went out toward the garden. The bustling in the kitchen began again, behind him.

"Wake up!" cried Mrs. Martinelli to the kitchen maid. "Get the pepper sauce for that Bandini devil. Fan that charcoal and bring it to life. Do something! What's the matter with you?"

Maria looked at her with wide, dark eyes.

"You were right," she said. "There will be a killing. And Bandini will be the dead man!"

Then she fell to her work again.

But out in the garden, there never was a more tranquil face than that of Silvertip as he passed under the high grape arbors until he found a small corner table. All the rest of the little garden was filled with family groups, Americans, flavoring their food with hearty portions of the red, home-made wine of Martinelli. No one paid any attention to Silvertip as he passed. Americans lack the public curiosity of the Latins, and only unhappiness makes them aware of the outside world. A contented party is surrounded by an impenetrable wall of its own pleasure, as it were, and that wall is rarely peered over. So those ranchers, miners, town tradesmen and shopkeepers of Cruces, with their families about them, talked high or low, and paid no heed to Silvertip as he went by.

He, apparently, had no more eye for them, and yet he studied every face in turn, analyzed it, shaved a mustache here to see if the naked skin might bring out a dangerous likeness; put on a beard there for the same reason. By the time he had reached his corner table, he was fairly well convinced that he knew none of them, and that none of them knew him.

Still, as he sat down, he was by no means willing to relax. He measured the height of the wall behind him.

14

He regarded the thickness of the arbor foliage, behind which a man might easily hide.

For Bandini was near, and Bandini would kill him by courage or by craft, if possible.

Antonio Martinelli came hobbling on his crippled leg. He embraced one of Silvertip's hands in both of his. He leaned over Silver's table, and beamed upon him.

"How are things?" said Silvertip.

"How can anything be bad with me? How can I ever complain?" said Martinelli. "I have a leg and a half, instead of no legs at all. Therefore we all thank God and Silvertip every day of our lives. Look! Here is the wine. If it is not beautiful, every drop, you shall have the blood out of my heart."

Silvertip made him sit down at the table. They tried the wine together, Martinelli smacking his lips.

"What's happening in there between Bandini and his friend?" asked Silvertip.

"It's no friend that's with Bandini," said Martinelli. "All I know is that Bandini wants something out of that young Mexican, and can't get it. But there'll be trouble! There'll be trouble!"

"I think so, too," said Silvertip, with a voice filled with quiet meaning. "I wish you'd watch and listen as much as you can. And let me know if a break seems to be coming on."

"You would help? You would stop the trouble?" asked Martinelli. "You know what one gun fight does—it spoils the name of a place. It takes away the cheerfulness. If people say: 'Martinelli's, where the man was killed the other day'—if they say that, they will come to me no more. I'll go and watch them like a hawk. I would give twenty dollars to have them under my eye as well as under my ear. I can only hear mumblings through the door, and very few words."

He went off, and Maria came, bearing a plate, the grated cheese, the Bolognese sauce, and a great platter of spaghetti. She put all the dishes down, deftly, and arranged them without making a clatter, and yet all the time her thoughtful eyes were on the face of Silvertip, not on her automatic work.

She paused one instant, watching Silvertip lift from the

15

platter the first white-dripping forkful of spaghetti and bring it over to his plate.

"You think of him still," said the girl. "But he will not harm you if you keep away from him."

She hurried away, as though frightened by her own boldness in giving an opinion, and the hazel-gray eyes of Silvertip watched her out of sight, before he moved his hand again.

He finished the spaghetti slowly. The goodness of the food to one who had eaten little except meat for many weeks, filled him again with that sleepy content against which he had to be so on guard. Finally he roused himself, as Martinelli came hobbling up the path, ducking under the trailing green of the arbor.

His face beamed a brighter red than before, as he exclaimed: "It is all finished; it is all well; and they're in the saloon drinking together like brothers!"

"Are they?" said Silvertip. "Then the trouble is right on the verge of breaking. I know the sort of brotherhood there is in Bandini!"

He looked at his watch. It was nine thirty.

He finished his wine with a gulp, and rising from the table, with a swift, secret gesture he touched the revolver that hung under his coat. Martinelli gaped vaguely at the form that strode so quickly before him, and started to hobble in pursuit.

But Silvertip entered the barroom far ahead. One glance showed him that Bandini was not there, in the long irregular line of noisy drinkers. He called the bartender with a crooking of his forefinger.

"Bandini?" he said.

"Bandini's just gone out with a young fellow, a friend who—"

Silvertip waited to hear no more. He felt sure that the young fellow was now indeed in grave danger, so he slipped out of the swinging doors onto the street. He whipped that street from end to end with a rapid glance, and saw the mere fluttering of a cloak as a man passed from view. Bandini, after all, was awaiting him in the street!

That was enough for Silvertip. He ran like a greyhound to that corner. A dark, narrowly winding alley moved

16

away on his left. He winced back a little from that darkness, as a kennel terrier might wince from the black tunnel of a fox's earth. Then he hurried straight forward, stepping long and light, every nerve in his body made acute, every sense working with electric surety and speed.

Something moved before him. Heels ground against the earth. He saw the swaying of a cloak, dimly seen through the shadows.

"Are you ready?" cried Silvertip. "Then fill your hand!"

The form whirled toward him, the cloak fanning well out to the side. One hand rose, as if to let go with the gun it seemed to hold. The other did not rise.

"Take it then, damn you!" muttered Silvertip, and drawing, he fired.

The finger of red fire flicked out of the muzzle of the gun, as though pointing the way for the bullet with the death it carried. That flash showed Silvertip not the face of Bandini, but a dark-skinned, handsome youth. The horror in those wide eyes flashed at Silvertip for an instant, and then the inflooding darkness covered the falling body.

Silvertip could not move; he could not catch that weight before it struck solidly against the ground. The dust that puffed out under the impact rose in a cloud, acrid against the nostrils of Silvertip.

He kneeled and put his hand over the heart of the fallen body. There was no beat. The coat was wet and warm with blood.

Silvertip, still kneeling, lifted his head as though to listen, but he was not heeding any human sound, far or near. He had killed the man he would have protected. A vow was forming in his heart, filling his throat.

CHAPTER III

Cross and Snake Brand

WHEN Silvertip rose, he was carrying the loose weight of the body in his arms. He felt the sway of the hanging head, the swinging of the feet with every step he took. There was still the warmth of life coming out of the body. The weight made his own step loud and heavy, like the footfall of a stranger, to his ear; and already his heart was heavier, too, with the double burden which he had taken upon himself.

He rounded to the rear of the restaurant of Martinelli, and through a side door carried the dead man straight into the small room where, only a few minutes before, this youth and Bandini had been at dinner. Two crumpled napkins lay on the table, now, and a scattering of soiled dishes, and glasses dimly stained by wine.

He put the body down in a chair. The form sagged helplessly against him, the head hanging, the arms dropping straight down toward the floor. Still supporting the inert thing, he cleared half the table with a few sweeps of his arm; then he laid out the young Mexican in the free space.

The puncture in the coat was a neat little round hole. There was not much blood anywhere on his clothing.

He straightened the legs and the arms. They did not seem to lie naturally along the side, so he folded them across the stomach of the dead man. The lips were still parted, as though in a gasp; the eyes of horror stared upward, unwinkingly, at the ceiling.

A footfall paused at the door; then Mrs. Martinelli's scream rose in shrill, endless waves that cut ceaselessly through his whirling brain.

Other people came, running. He regarded them not at all. He closed the eyes, and they remained closed. He touched the tip of the chin, still soft and warm, and brought the lips together.

It was as though he had dragged the soul of the dead man up from hell to heaven, for it was a faintly smiling face, a happy, dreaming face. He was not more, this handsome young Mexican, than twenty or twenty-two; and the features were beautifully carved. There was strength and manliness in the face, also; and Silvertip felt that Fate, with sinister malice, had driven his bullet into one of the chosen men of the earth. If there had been a garden of weeds with one priceless flower blooming, he, like a blind gardener, had felled the once choice plant.

In a hundred years of striving, what could he do for the world that would equal the value of the life he had canceled?

Silvertip, stirring from his dream, took a handkerchief, and wiped the dust from the black, silky hair. There was still warmth in the brow, also. With every touch it seemed to Silvertip that the life could not actually have gone, that the forward running of the years could not have ended, as a river ends at the sea.

Silvertip himself was not so many years the senior of this dead man, yet he felt like an old man beside a child.

What would that child have grown into? Upon what labors would it have set its hands?

He regarded the soft, slender tapering of the fingers— far unlike his own hands.

And now, as he looked down at the still face, he laid his grip on the two hands which he had joined, and groaned.

Some great purpose burns in every soul; if only he could penetrate into the dead mystery of that mind, he swore, in that solemnity of silence, that he would undertake the unfinished labor of this life.

A voice broke in upon him. He looked up. People were staring at him, not at the dead man, for there was something in the face of Silver that filled them with awe.

It was the sheriff speaking.

"Silvertip, can you tell us about this?"

"I found the dead body in the alley one block down from the restaurant," said Silvertip.

"Bandini!" cried the voice of young Piero Martinelli. "José Bandini was with him all the evening, right here in this room. Bandini did it."

"Bandini?" said the sheriff. "Where is he?"

"Not Bandini," said Silvertip firmly. "I saw him going down the street a minute or two before the shot was fired. It certainly wasn't Bandini."

"No," said the bartender. "It couldn't have been Bandini. He may have been arguing with this poor kid, but he stopped the arguing before they left the barroom. I seen them make up and shake hands. I seen Bandini go and take off his cloak and put it around the shoulders of this dead kid. I seen him do it, kind of like a gift, to show that he meant to be friends, honest and straight."

Silvertip looked up, slowly, into the eyes of the bartender. The trick of Bandini had been too simple for belief. By that simple change of dress he had made another man walk in his own footsteps to meet a death that should have been his own.

It was not just chance that had killed this victim. It was not the hand of Silvertip, either, though he had fired the shot. It was Bandini's craft that had performed the murder!

Silvertip drew in a great, slow breath.

The sheriff said again, slowly: "Silver, I know that it ain't like you to be shootin' gents in dark alleys. It ain't your style or your cut. But you've used guns, plenty. Where was you, all the evening?"

"He was in there in the barroom," said the bartender. "When the gun went off, I heard the shot. I heard it, but I didn't think much about it. Silvertip hadn't hardly got through the door."

Silvertip looked into the broad, red face of the bartender and silently thanked him for that lie.

"It's goin' to be one of them mysteries," said the sheriff sadly. "We don't even know who he is. Does anybody here know who he is?"

No one knew. So the sheriff started a careful examination of the pockets.

They revealed very little. There was a small pearl-handled pocket-knife which made some of the men smile a little. There was a little .32-caliber revolver of a bulldog model that would fit neatly into almost any pocket. There was a bill fold containing a hundred and forty-seven dollars. There was a gold watch of a fine Swiss make, with a delicately worked gold chain that had been simply dropped into the pocket that held the watch.

The sheriff pried open the back of the watch, examined it with care, and replaced it with the little heap of belongings.

He turned his baffled eyes upon Silvertip.

"Silver," he said, "you look kind of cut up. Wasn't he a friend of yours?"

"No," said Silvertip. "He's just so young—that's all!" He added: "Have you looked at his horse?"

They trooped out to the stable and found the horse. It was a high-headed queen of a mare, a blood bay with four black silk stockings on her legs and eyes like liquid diamonds that turned and shone in the lantern light. On one of her quarters was burned a cross with a wavering line under it.

"That's the Cross and Snake brand of old Arturo Monterey, down in the Haverhill River country," said the sheriff. "I know that brand! Maybe down there I could pick up a clew to the name of this gent. Why, it's a fifty-mile ride."

Silvertip touched the sheriff's shoulder.

"I'll go," he said. "I've never been down there, but I know the way. I'll take the outfit of that poor fellow; I'll take his horse along, too."

"Would the outfit and the horse arrive if you started with 'em?" asked the sheriff tersely.

Then, under the steady eye and the faint smile of Silvertip, he flushed.

21

"I didn't mean that. It just sort of come popping out," he explained. "Silver, no matter what some say about you, I'll trust you around the world and back. When will you start?"

"Now," said Silvertip.

"You mean in the morning?"

"I mean—now!"

The sheriff nodded slowly. "Something about this job has sort of burned you up, Silver, eh? Take the lot and start now, then, if you want to. Find old Arturo Monterey if you can. They say he's a hard case; I dunno in what way. But find out if he remembers selling a hoss like this to anybody, and the name of the hombre that got it. That's all. Then you'll come back here and let me know?"

"I'll come back," said Silvertip.

He was lifting his saddle off a peg as he spoke, and the sheriff, after pausing for a last glance at his messenger, went back to the restaurant and the dead body, the curious crowd following him. Only the red-faced bartender remained.

"I would have been in the soup," Silvertip told him curtly. "Thanks for that lie."

"You did the job, eh?" said the bartender, leaning against the manger on one hand and peering into the face of Silver.

"I did the job."

"Thinking it was Bandini?"

"Yes."

The bartender nodded his head slowly. "A kind of an idea come over me," he said. "A kind of an idea that there was a dirty trick in the brain of Bandini when he give that kid his cloak. He ain't the kind that gives something for nothing."

"You saved my neck," said Silver.

"That's all right," said the bartender. "But I'd kind of like to ask you a question."

"Anything you like."

"You got something in your mind, Silver. What's dragging you down into that hell hole, the Haverhill?"

"Because there's a brand on the boy's horse; and the brand come out of the Haverhill Valley, they say."

"Yeah, that's all right. But there's something more on

your mind than that. What's on your mind, Silver?"

"I've killed a man," said Silver.

"According to yarns, he ain't the first."

"I've had fights with men who were born with guns in their hands," said Silvertip. "I've fought in the dark, too, as far as that goes. But this was no fight. It wasn't murder, either. There can't be a murder except when there's murder in your mind. I was sure he had drawn on me. What was it, then?"

"It was just a kind of a wiping out of the poor young gent," suggested the bartender.

"I wiped him out," said Silvertip slowly. "And by the look of him, he was a better man than I'll ever be. What can I do? Two things, partner, and, by heavens, I'm going to do them!"

"Two things?" said the bartender.

"If I can find out his name and the lives that he fitted into, I can find out at the same time what he was meant to do in the world. By the look of him, that would be something too fine for my hands. But whatever his job was, I can *try* to do it, partner."

The bartender shrugged.

"I see what you mean, Silver," said he. "And a doggone strange thing it seems to me. Now, supposing that this here gent, maybe, has got a wife and a coupla brats stowed away somewhere? What would you do? Marry the widow?"

"Work for her and the youngsters," said Silvertip solemnly, "till I rubbed the flesh off the bones of my hands."

"Would you?" said the bartender. "Well, you beat me. But that ain't queer. You beat most people. Well, that's the first thing you wanta do. Mind telling me the second?"

"I'll tell you," said Silvertip, through his teeth, and suddenly in a cold rage. "You ought to be able to guess, though."

"I know," agreed the bartender, "Bandini is the bird that fixed up this job on you. You never would 'a' picked out the kid for a gun play except that he was wearing the cloak—and Bandini must 'a' known that. Are you going after him?"

"Before I die," said Silvertip, "I'll see Bandini in front of me, and I'll get at him with a gun or a knife or my bare hands."

"Yeah," said the bartender. "You will! I can see it like a picture in a book. Silver, I'm goin' to wish you luck. You're a cut different from all the rest of us—but I'm goin' to wish you luck. But fit yourself into the skin of another gent's life? Man, man, nobody in the world ever had an idea like that!"

That was all he said before he went out from the barn.

Silvertip, in the meantime, finished saddling and bridling. He saddled and bridled the bay mare, also, and tied her lead rope to his pommel. Then he brought the two horses out into the open and mounted.

He wanted, above all else, to go back into the restaurant and look once more at the delicate, olive-skinned beauty of that dead face, but he kept that impulse in check.

He gathered the reins for the start; inside the house he could hear the high-pitched, excited voice of Mrs. Martinelli, babbling out her woes.

The broncho moved suddenly and set jingling all the possessions of the dead man, which the sheriff had poured into one of the saddlebags. So Silvertip rode from Cruces into the night.

CHAPTER IV

The Haverhill Country

IT WAS early morning when he got through the Haverhill Pass and looked down along the valley of the Haverhill River. As far as his eye could reach, from the height, the bright water was running in wide, sweeping curves, silver-clear just below him, and a dull-blue sheen far off, with winkings of high lights on it now and then.

Men had told him that there was a curse on this country, and, in fact, he had always heard strange tales of it. So had every one. Very few exact reports came through, but there were mysterious murmurings. Now and then some one was pointed out as a "Haverhill man," and that fellow was sure to be avoided by all other people on the range. At least, until he had proved himself anew.

There was always talk about the Haverhill country, yet it was odd that so few people had accurate knowledge. It was not simply that the high mountains encircled it. Mountains cannot fence any place from a Westerner. But those who went into the valley seldom came out, and if they did, they were not easily drawn into talk. One might have thought that it was a hellish place—but never had Silvertip looked on pleasanter country.

There was plenty of water, for one thing. He had ridden up out of a plain where the grass was all dust-gray, but what he looked on now was a soft green comfort to the eye. And from the highlands on both sides he had glimpses of brooks running silver and white down the slopes to the Haverhill River below. Moreover, there were trees. There were big, roundheaded trees in groves that hung against the more brilliant green of the grass hillsides like dark clouds against the blue sheen of the sky. A heavenly place altogether, he decided. Nothing but gossip could poison it.

He made a cigarette, lighted it, began to inhale smoke in great whiffs.

He laughed, threw his hat in the air, and caught it again in spite of the frantic dodging and bucking of the mustang beneath him. He had changed from saddle to saddle all the way during the night. The horses were still fresh, especially that deer-shaped, wing-footed bay mare; so he made no longer halt, but rode down the trail toward the little village that lay at the side of the stream in the central valley beneath.

The trail was very winding, and he never could endure to push a horse going downhill. It meant ruined shoulders too often. So it was nearly prime of the morning before he came off the trail onto a beaten road near the town.

A man in a buckboard came past him from the village. Silvertip lifted his hat and called good morning:

The fellow kept his reins in one hand and his stub of a buggy whip in the other. He kept jerking at the reins constantly, and tapping at the down-headed span of mustangs with the other, without in the slightest degree altering their gait. He returned no salute or gesture or word. The wind tipped the brim of his felt hat up and down, but there was not even a nod of actual greeting.

Silver turned in the saddle and looked back. The stranger had turned also, and was staring. He was a gaunt man, of late middle age. The stubble of his beard gave a gray sheen to his face. His eyes were set in dark hollows. It was a craggy face. It was to the faces of other men as a rocky upland farm is to the rich green acres of a smooth river bottom.

At length Silver faced the town again, frowning. He had been through a great part of the West, and he had been through it on horseback or on foot. He had used his eyes, too, simply because he *had* to use them to save his scalp. But he could never remember encountering behavior like this.

All that he had heard of the Haverhill country swept over his mind again like clouds across a sunny day.

He rode on at a walk, because he wanted to digest this town as well as he could with his eyes before he entered it.

It looked like any of a thousand other Western villages. There were the same flimsy shacks that seemed to have been thrown together at random—mere tents to be occupied by an army that would soon pass on. For Westerners have had something to do other than lavish time on places to eat and sleep and sit. They have had business to do, and their business has been the whole outdoors.

This was like all the rest, in so far as Silvertip could see, and there was little that his keen eye missed. He hunted every board, every shingle, every window like a hawk searching for game.

As he came into the single winding street, he heaved a sigh of relief. Everything was the same. The signs in front of the shops, and the stores, and the hotel, and the saloons —all were the true Western pattern.

Then he saw a small boy of eight standing in an open doorway with a grown-up's shotgun in his hands.

"Hello, son!" called Silvertip.

The boy made no answer. He turned his grave face to stare after Silvertip, but he spoke not a word, made not a gesture. It was a broad, roughly made face with an expression far older than the possible years. And the eyes were set in deep hollows filled with shadow!

The chill struck again through the blood and up the spinal marrow of Silvertip.

Men may be different in varying parts of the world, but the children should all be the same.

Then he heard the cheerful beating of hammers on an anvil. Yonder was a blacksmith's shop with horses tethered before it, waiting to be shod. And through the open doors drifted thin puffs of blue coal smoke.

Silvertip breathed more easily again. The noise of the hammers rejoiced him, at that moment, as much as the sound of human voices could have done.

He halted in front of the shop, dismounted, and looked inside. A cow-puncher sat just inside the door, making a cigarette as he sat on an upturned tempering tub. The elderly blacksmith was holding a bar of iron with a large pair of pincers, and as he turned it and tapped it with his light hammer, a powerful striker banged on the indicated spots with a twelve-pound sledge.

The head blacksmith spoke two words, or three—no more. And then both turned full on Silvertip. He saw their faces were broad, their eyes set in deep, shadowy hollows!

CHAPTER V

The Silent Men

THERE had been something of a nightmare ghastliness about the passing of that farmer down the road silently, and the sight of that silent lad on the porch, gun in hand, silent, also. But now the dreamlike quality departed from the scene and left to Silvertip a most absolute sense of reality. A grim reality, but one with the full sun of truth playing on it. He had simply run into a backward lot of sour men who had migrated, no doubt, from some single section of the East or of the Old World, and had developed a common surliness of manner just as they had grown to be similar in features. That cow-puncher who sat by the door, at least, was a distinct type. He was small, wizened, with a birdlike beak of a nose and birdlike eyes. But there was no more friendliness in him than in the others.

"Morning to you all," said Silvertip cheerfully.

A nod of greeting is an inclination of the head; the head blacksmith merely jerked his up a trifle. His striker did not move at all. Their heavy, obstinate, unlighted eyes weighed down upon the face of Silvertip in silence.

. He ran on briskly: "I've got a mare out there with a brand that I've heard called the Cross and Snake brand. I've heard that the brand comes out of this valley. Is that right?"

He was incredulous when silence greeted this direct question. Anger burned up in him with a gust, like flame through dry tinder. He mastered it at once. He had learned, by hard lessons, that a quick temper must not be allowed to flare—no, never!

However, there is such a thing as standing up for one's rights. And he said coldly: "I asked a question. Did any of you hear me?"

He smiled as he said that. There was something about that smile of Silver's that cut like a knife edge through the most obdurate stupidity and the most sullen resentment. It never failed to point his words.

The elder blacksmith jerked a thumb toward the cowpuncher who sat by the door.

"You talk to him, Ed," he said.

The little man by the door pushed back his sombrero, scratched his head until a bushy forelock fell down across his eyes, lighted a cigarette, threw the match away, inhaled and exhaled the first smoke cloud.

"I dunno much about brands here," said Ed.

"Well," answered Silvertip, "suppose you come out and take a look, partner?"

"I dunno that looking would do much good," said Ed. "I ain't a brand expert."

He became aware, then, of the small, cold smile of Silvertip, and rose slowly to his feet.

"Ain't any harm in taking a look, I guess," said he.

He stood by the mare. The sight of the brand did not seem sufficient to him. He had to run a forefinger across the lines of it. Then he had to thumb up the gloss of the hair to see the print of the scars on the hide.

At last he stood back and shook his head.

"Never saw that brand before?" asked Silvertip.

."A man sees a lot of brands here and there," said Ed, looking at his cigarette.

"How long have you been living in Haverhill Valley?"

"Why, quite a spell," said Ed.

"What do you mean by 'quite a spell'?" asked Silvertip.

"Why, quite a heap," said Ed.

"Oh, you've stayed here quite a heap, have you? Ever heard of a Mexican called Arturo Monterey?"

"Arturo Monterey?" asked Ed, looking still at the fuming point of his cigarette.

"Yes, Arturo Monterey."

"Well, it seems to me," remarked Ed, "that I've heard the name somewheres. I ain't well acquainted around Haverhill Valley."

He turned and walked back into the blacksmith shop slowly, dragging the heels of his boots in the dust, and sat down again in the shadow within the door.

Silvertip took a deep breath and let curses flow out silently with the exhalation. It was a new experience for him. He had been through many difficult times, and through many dangers among savage and brutal men; but he had never been badgered like this before. Something about him usually prevented light treatment at the hands of others.

He went back to the door of the blacksmith shop and made for himself a new cigarette. The clangor of the hammers on the iron had recommenced, and every beat of the metal on metal sent a savage pulse through his body and through his brain.

Slowly he made the cigarette, and slowly he lighted it.

He was aware—as if through the back of his head—that Ed had smiled at the blacksmith, and that the blacksmith had smiled at Ed. The poison of anger invaded every portion of Silvertip's being.

And yet his hands were tied. Besides, he had been forewarned. Men had told him that there was danger and death in the very air of the Haverhill Valley. He could understand that now. He had a strong feeling, amounting to surety, that if he attempted to discipline any one of these three, they would all be at him, like so many wolves of a pack. No matter what else could be said of them, they seemed all capable of giving a good account of themselves with their hands. They were made to endure shocks and to give them.

So he stood there, trying to think, but unable to connect one idea with another.

And then he told himself, suddenly and grimly, that this

31

was as it should be. He was trying to find the unfinished life of a dead man and complete it, and therefore every step of the way, from the beginning, was sure to be hard. It was better so. Only with pain could he pay his debt, and far bitterer pain than this must be his before the end.

Ed stood up presently, and sauntered out of the shop and up the street. A butcher—wearing the badge of a red-stained apron—walked out with a bucket of slops, which he threw into the dust of the street. It made a great black triangle of mud in the midst of the white. Ed paused by him, spoke to him. And the butcher turned sharply around to stare at Silvertip.

Then he laughed.

That whip cut made Silvertip tremble as though a cold wind had struck him.

Ed and the butcher went into the shop door together, the butcher still laughing. The sound of his laughter came braying down the street even when he was inside his shop again.

Silver turned his head. The blacksmith was grinning, too. He looked steadily back at Silver, all the while busy with both hands at his work, and continued to grin. Silver glanced quickly back at the street.

Out of the distance a sound of a herd of cattle driven on a narrow trail had been growing, a thunder of lowing mingled with sharp, clashing sounds, such as horns make against horns, or splay hoofs clacking together. Now the river of noise entered the street, was confined by the houses, and doubled and redoubled suddenly.

He looked back and saw the swaying fronts of the steers coming, big, wide-shouldered, deep-bodied animals. Two Mexicans rode before them, slender, graceful fellows with enormous hats set over the darkness of their faces. They rode proudly, as all Mexicans ride.

They went by. The steers followed. The wide wash of that crowded herd almost scraped against fences and posts on either side of the roadway. They came in a thin smother of dust, like a blowing sea mist that rolls over the waves. Silvertip saw the red shining of the eyes, the sheen of the long, lyre-shaped horns, the glistening of the wet noses.

They were fat, these great brutes. They showed the green grass they had been battening on. Rolls of heavy

32

flesh were bouncing up and down their flanks. Their tails swung like great flails. They beat up a clashing uproar with their feet, and the dust squirted out in thickening clouds.

But in a moment more Silvertip saw something else to take his eye. For on one of the quarters of every one of these animals there was the big pattern of a very distinct brand—a cross with a wavering line beneath it!

This was the brand about which Ed was not sure—not sure whether he had seen it or not—not sure that it belonged to the herds of Arturo Monterey or no!

He turned and saw the blacksmiths laughing in unison, boldly, openly, laughing Silvertip to scorn, laughing in his very face. And still he controlled himself.

The end of the herd poured past in thick dust masses; the mouths of the steers were hanging open; they crowded against those in the lead, just like fish swarming in a shoal. Close behind them came more riders.

Silvertip stepped out through the billowing mist and waved his hand before a rider. The man drew up with a jerk. His gray-powdered face turned impatiently toward the questioner.

"Partner," said Silvertip, "I want to know where I can find the house of Arturo Monterey?"

The teeth of the Mexican flashed.

"Gringo swine!" he yelled, and sent his mustang ahead again with a slash of the quirt.

Silver turned, and saw that the blacksmith and his helper were both standing in the door of the shop, swaying with delighted laughter.

Another rider galloped up the street, the last of the lot. Silver sprang before him with raised hand.

The horse dodged.

"Out of my way, gringo!" yelled the Mexican with a curse.

The refined steel of Silvertip's patience parted with a snap. With one long bound he reached that Mexican's side and caught him by the wrist and the collar. The speed of the horse did the rest. It tore the Mexican from his saddle and rolled him with Silvertip in the deepness of the dust.

Something winked before Silver's eyes. He reached at the flash and caught the wrist of the Mexican's knife hand.

33

One twist and the knife dropped. Silver stood up, lifting the cow-puncher with him. Dust poured down like water from the clothes of both of them. The roar of the herd departed; the shouted laughter of the blacksmiths began to predominate.

Suddenly that laughter had increased, not diminished in volume, and Silvertip was more bewildered than ever. Was it a common thing to the people of these parts to see a dashing Mexican caballero, a man with the shoulders of a bull, plucked from his horse and disarmed as he drew a knife?

He laid the point of that knife against the shirt of the herdsman.

"Now, amigo," said Silvertip, "we talk."

The Mexican glanced over his shoulder at the diminishing cloud of dust that was the herd. And Silver could read the thought. How long before the fellow's companions saw a riderless horse coming after them and turned back to learn the fate of their companion?

"We talk," said Silvertip. "I ask you, first, if the Cross and Snake brand belongs, really, to Arturo Monterey?"

The vaquero stared into his face with eyes yellow and red-stained by fury. He said nothing.

"Tell me," said Silver.

The body of the Mexican was shaking with rage. His hands kept flexing and unflexing.

"Yes," he said at last.

"Very well," said Silver. "And where is the house of Monterey?"

Even fear of the knife could not prevent the Mexican from shouting savagely: "In it's own place, gringo!"

And he swayed forward a little, as though expecting the thrust of the knife.

"Look at that bay mare," said Silvertip. "Did you ever see her before?"

The Mexican glanced at the high-headed beauty. His eyes widened; his jaw dropped; his very color changed, it seemed to Silvertip. Then the big head of the man swung back, and he scowled at his questioner.

It was plain to Silvertip that he had reached the end of the rope, that he could extract no more words from this fellow. It was equally plain that the mare was known to the Mexican intimately. Yet it seemed that all the men of the Haverhill Valley would rather die, almost, than talk.

"All right, hombre," said Silvertip, and tossed the knife to him carelessly. The Mexican caught it out of the air with a hungry hand. He had the air, for an instant, of one about to leap forward; but again there was something in the faint smile and the steady eyes of Silvertip that discouraged attack. Presently the big man turned and strode off down the street, making violent gestures, cursing volubly to himself.

The two blacksmiths had stopped their laughter. They remained in the doorway and watched with brutally inexpressive faces while Silver remounted and rode down the street to a hotel. He found stable room behind the place; when he entered the hotel itself, a lowering clerk seemed unwilling to give him a room at first, but eventually he was shown to a dingy corner apartment that overlooked a side lane and the back yard. There he sat down and took his head between his hands. He was sleepy from his all-night ride, but the jumping of his nerves kept him from lying down.

He was half beaten within an hour of his arrival in the Haverhill Valley. All the self-confidence had melted from him, and he felt that he was leaning the weight of his mind against an impenetrable wall.

CHAPTER VI

The House of Monterey

HE STRETCHED on the bed at last, for he could find no solution to his problem, and he knew that he needed sleep. When he wakened, a few hours later, a whispering air fanned his face, and he saw the door slowly swinging open.

When it was wide, Silvertip was already sitting up, at watch, and he observed on the threshold a man whose face was of the brutal type which he had seen so often before this in the Haverhill Valley. He was making a cigarette, leaning one shoulder against the jamb, and dripping tobacco unconcernedly over the floor. He was big, like most of these Haverhill men; and, like the rest of them, he stared heavily and steadily, without a shift in his eyes.

"You're the gent that slammed Juan Perez, are you?" asked the stranger.

"Who are you, brother?" asked Silvertip.

"Chuck Terry. Alligator sent me down to get you."

"Get me for what?" asked Silvertip.

"For the ranch."

"I'm not looking for a job."

"Sure you ain't," agreed "Chuck" Terry. "The job's

looking for you. Grade-A pay, and the best eats in the land. Is that the sort of a picture you wanta step into?'

Silvertip stood up.

"Look here," said he. "Who's the Alligator? I never heard of him."

Chuck Terry came suddenly to life, stepped into the room, and closed the door behind him.

"You never heard of Alligator Hank?" he repeated. "You never heard of Drummon?"

"No," said Silver. "Never heard of either of 'em."

With amazement, with long-drawn-out disgust, Chuck Terry regarded him.

"Well, what's the use, then?" said Chuck. "What're you driving at in the valley, anyway? You slam a greaser, and yet you ain't throwing in with Drummon?"

"Should I?" asked Silvertip.

"You know your own business better'n I do," replied Chuck Terry.

"What I want to do, first of all," said Silvertip, "is to find the place of Arturo Monterey."

This announcement was so interesting to Terry that he came a step or two closer to Silver, peering earnestly at him all the time.

"You wanta find out where Monterey lives?" he asked.

"I've asked a lot of people already," said Silvertip, "and they laugh at me."

Terry himself began to grin.

"All right," he answered. "I'll tell you. You want to see Monterey, do you? Well, ride right on down the valley and take the first road that forks over to the left. Keep down that left fork till you sight a house that looks like a dog-gone old castle out of a fairy-story book. And somewheres around there, likely you'll run into this gent, this Arturo Monterey, all right."

Terry struggled with a grin that would not be totally suppressed. It worked and twisted at his face.

"So long, brother," he said. "You go and find Don Arturo."

And, striding to the door, Terry cast it wide, slammed it behind him, and hurried down the hall. A noise of suppressed laughter, then a roar of it, came echoing back to Silvertip.

He went to the window and looked out at the brightness of the day, at the roofs of the town with quivering heat waves dancing over them, and beyond were the muscular knees of the mountains and their bare upward shoulders. For the first time since his childhood he felt the cold fear of this physical world reach him and finger his very heart. He seemed to have entered a region of ironical Titans. Among them he was reduced to an absurdity, and that purpose which had brought him to the place became more dreamlike than ever.

But his trail, he was sure, would take him far out of the Haverhill Valley. If he felt like a stranger in the place, it was certain that the slender fellow he had killed could never have lived here. It was merely to pick up some clew of him and then to be gone on the out trail that Silver lingered in Haverhill Valley. And with all his heart, he yearned to be gone at once!

He went down to the stable, saddled his own mustang and the mare, and rode down the street with grinning faces at watch on either side of him. They knew where he was going. They knew all about it. And they foresaw disaster, which pleased them to the heart. A group of boys tumbling in a vacant lot jumped up and shouted and pointed at him. Even the children understood things that were curtained away from his understanding.

He was glad to be out of that town, as if escaping from a curse, into the green, open arms of the country. The bright running of the river washed away some of the shadows that were pouring up in his mind. To his desert-bred eyes, the green undulations of the valley were more than waves of gold, and peace came to him as he watched the cattle grazing or lying in dim shadows under the trees. The strength flowed back, and that self-confidence which never had been lost to him for so many years until he entered the town of Haverhill.

He found the branching road that ran to the left. It was worn more by hoofs than wheels, and it mounted into the throat of a narrow valley. Great walls of rock went straight up on either side, one blue with shadow, one on fire with the sun, and through the middle of the canyon a creek ran with a sound of rushing, like a wind. The way up the valley was half blocked by the house of Arturo Monterey.

He knew it by Terry's description, for the road wound up a steep slope toward the entrance; on the other side was a precipitous fall of rocks, and above rose old adobe walls and one blunt tower of stone.

Up the winding way, Silvertip came to the house itself, and a great stone arch across the entrance to the patio. A big Mexican appeared suddenly and stood in his way. Silvertip dismounted.

"Amigo," he said, "I've come up here to find out, if I can, if Señor Monterey ever owned this horse, and who he sold it to. Maybe you can tell me and save me a lot of trouble?"

The Mexican regarded him with a long side glance in silence. Then he turned toward the mare with a sudden start, as though there were something about the animal which had jarred home upon his memory.

"Wait!" he said to Silver, and hurried back into the patio.

Silvertip looked curiously about him. Chuck Terry's description had been a little from the point; the place was more like a fortress than a castle, and the weather-worn dobe had the look of immense age. The patio was flagged with great stones and surrounded by an arching arcade, under the shadow of which he could see doors of heavy oak. The faces of those doors were seamed and cracked by dry old age.

His Mexican reappeared now, and not alone. Two other men walked briskly through the entrance arch, went by Silvertip, then halted suddenly. The man to whom he had spoken came up more slowly, with the look of a hunter who has marked down prey. A door opened on the farther side of the patio; more footsteps approached; and Silver knew that he was trapped.

White men or Mexicans, the Haverhill Valley seemed to be filled with madmen! He glanced over his shoulder toward the first pair who had passed through the arch; they faced him now, one with a drawn gun, one with his hand on a revolver butt. He thought of mounting and trying to break through, and cast that hope away even as it entered his mind.

Two newcomers loomed now at the side of the patio entrance. One of those he knew by the bull face and the sleek round of the neck, that same fellow whom he had pulled from a horse that morning, and to whom Terry had given the name of Juan Perez. He opened eyes and mouth, then grinned gapingly with joy.

"The gringo!" he cried, and reached for his gun.

Retreat was thoroughly blocked; Silvertip followed his normal instinct by advancing. He jumped like a scared cat at his first interlocutor, who had called out all this show of strength against him. The fellow's face convulsed, reaching for a weapon.

"Stop!" cried a woman's voice. "Juan Perez, stop!"

Nothing could have nullified the motion which Perez had begun. There was a Colt already in the hand of Silver, but he held fire, and saw the fingers of Perez open, so that the revolver he had drawn flicked away and went spinning and rattling and slithering over the pavement of the patio.

Other guns were burning in the keen sunlight all around Silver. If he had been in danger before in his life, it was never a greater danger than that which surrounded him now. The voice of the woman had saved him. The mellow sound of her words still lingered in his mind, tasted and retasted.

She had suspended all the murderous action that had been in progress.

Then Juan Perez was crying out as he turned to the side, gesticulating violently: "This is the man with the horse of Pedrillo! Look! Look for yourself, señorita!"

Past the arch of the entrance a girl came into view. She wore sandals and a wide-brimmed hat of cheap straw, like any peon woman, but her dress was the white translucency of fine linen, and there was a dark Latin beauty in her face. A careless glance might have passed her over in a crowd; but a second look would be sure to dwell on her, and little else.

She came straight toward Silver, and paused at a distance which maintained her dignity.

"What is your name?" she asked.

"Silver," said he.

He took off his hat before her. The brilliance of the sun struck a dazzle across his eyes. He put on his hat again and looked steadily at her through the protecting shadow that fell across his eyes.

"You have the horse of Pedro Monterey," said the girl. "How did it come to you?"

"He is dead," said Silver.

He heard them all cry out. He saw them all surge in toward him and stop again, as though his words had first drawn and then repelled them, as the edge of a cliff draws frightened men. Only the girl remained motionless and well poised, though he could see the pain had gone through her wide eyes and was still working in her.

He added: "I say that he's dead. I only know that the man who rode this horse was middle height, slender, handsome, dark, about twenty or twenty-two years old."

"That was Pedro Monterey," said the girl. "His father will see you."

She turned about. One of the vaqueros hurried to take her arm, but she paused and said in her distinct, quiet voice:

"I can walk very well by myself. Call the señor."

Then she passed out of view with the same unhurried step.

CHAPTER VII

Don Arturo

SILVER looked around on the stricken faces of the Mexicans who surrounded him. That sorrow was not strange to him, nor the blow which the girl had received so calmly and so deeply. It was right that the man he had killed should have come from such a place as this, with the air of a manor about it. Perhaps the girl was his sister, and these were the adherents of the house. The dead face had been that of an aristocrat, and it was from such a setting as this that he must have come. Long generations of breeding and culture will carve the features with more delicacy, and refine the body itself.

And the very soul of Silver expanded. If he had undertaken a great task, it was in a worthy cause. But more than ever he was baffled and bewildered. For how could he set his great hands to any task that had been important in the life of that dead man who now had a name—Pedro Monterey? Pedrillo, the vaqueros had called him, with an affectionate intonation.

They still pressed close, watching Silver like so many wolves about a helpless elk. He had put away his useless gun. Against such numbers it was a folly to show any sign of resistance. The least gesture in such a moment as this would bring the end of him, he knew that perfectly well.

He made a cigarette, lighted, and began to smoke it.

The news he brought had entered the house. These vaqueros who stood on guard about him had endured the shock steadily enough, but there were women in the big, sprawling house, and now voices rang out here and there in wild peals of grief that came through the walls as though through compressed lips.

The vaqueros began to be moved by those audible signs of woe. Some of them started swaying a little from side to side. Voices rose half audibly, bubbling and moaning, struggling in their throats, wordlessly.

But other words came. He heard them say: "The gringo!" and again: "The gringo dog! The dog!"

He was the messenger of bad news, and that was enough to insure him a bad reception. Lucky for him if the reaction consisted of words only.

The hinges of a heavy door grated. And then a slow footfall came across the patio.

"It is Don Arturo—God help him! God be merciful to him!" Silver heard one of the men murmur.

All of the Mexicans drew back a little, as though in respect, and in sympathy, while an old man with sweeping silver hair and a pointed gray beard came out into the patio. Time had pinched his shoulders a little, and perhaps it was the flow of hair that made the head seem disproportionately large. All his features were accented, together with the whiteness of his hair, by a band of black cloth which passed across his forehead, to be lost immediately under the flow of his hair. He would be a more imposing figure seated than standing; but even as he stood, he was a man of mark. He walked with a slim cane in his hand, his meager fingers spread out on the round head of it. And as he came to a halt, he stood very straight, as if at attention.

The blow had fallen on him, and, like the girl, he had received it calmly. The weight of it had not broken him. No doubt there was a deeper shadow under his brows now than there had been a few moments before. Perhaps his lips were pressed more tightly together. But his voice was calm as he said:

"You are Señor Silver?"

"I am," said Silver.

"You come to tell me that Pedro Monterey is dead?"

"The man who rode that horse—a young man—dark, handsome—" began Silver.

But the other lifted his hand.

"What was the manner of his dying, Señor Silver?" he asked.

The girl had come out from the house. She stood in the shadow of the arcade that surrounded the patio. One fold of her linen skirt thrust forward, and flashed like snow in the sunshine that touched it. She looked like the dead youth; she must be his sister, in fact. But what manner of people were these, when a father and sister could take the news of a death in such a way?

"May I speak to you alone?" said Silver.

Arturo Monterey drew himself up a little.

"In twenty years," he said, "no American has entered this house. May it be another hundred years before one of your race passes through my door. You stand in my patio; and even that is very much, indeed! But come closer to me, if you will. My sons, fall back."

The vaqueros moved off a little distance, their spurs rattling. Silver moved forward until he was close to the older Monterey. And just at that moment the opening of a door, as it seemed, allowed a wild cry of lament to break out from the house, a single dreadful note of grief, shut away to dimness again, as though the door had been suddenly closed once more.

Silver saw the chin of the old man jerk up, as he endured the thrust of that keening. But nothing seemed able really to shock Arturo Monterey.

"It was in Cruces," said Silver. "Do you know the place?"

Arturo Monterey made a slowly sweeping gesture.

"The mountains of the Haverhill," he said, "are the boundaries of my life."

"It's a small town," said Silver, "fifty miles from here, beyond the mountains. I was there, and I met an enemy of mine, who was with your son."

44

"What was his name?" asked Monterey.

"Bandini."

"Bandini is an enemy of yours?"

"So much so, that we agreed to meet at a certain hour, and fight out our arguments together. At that time, I went into the street to find him. I saw a man wearing Bandini's cloak. I followed him, and stopped him. Señor, a man does not pause to ask many questions, at such a time. I was sure that it was Bandini. I challenged him with enough words to give him a chance to draw a gun. It seemed to me that he drew. Then I pulled my gun and fired. And the fire that spurted out of the gun showed me not the face of Bandini, but that of a stranger. He fell dead! I took his horse and his possessions, and traced him through the horse to this house. And what I wish to say is—"

"Perez! Juan!" gasped Monterey.

He gripped his walking stick with both hands, and leaned a little on it.

"Take him!" groaned Monterey through his teeth, as the men came running to him. "Take the cursed gringo! God told me, twenty-five years ago, that nothing but evil could come to me from them, and here is another proof! Take him—away from my eyes—out of my sight—where I shall not hear the death cry! Make of him what my son is—a dead thing!"

They closed on Silver from either side, suddenly. Many pairs of hands gripped him with a force that ground the muscles against the bones, and paralyzed the nerves. In an instant he was as helpless as though he had lain for a month in benumbing fetters.

What a savage joy there was in their eyes, in the twisting of their mouths as they grasped and shook him! The grip of their fingers on his body seemed to feed them, like so many dogs tearing at living flesh.

And then he heard the girl calling out, not loudly: "Uncle Arturo, what are you doing?"

"I am finding justice, justice, justice on the gringo!" cried Arturo Monterey. "Quickly, my sons—quickly! Juan Perez, you will take charge, for you have seen this man before, and know a little about him. No torments—let death kill with a sharp edge, suddenly!"

There was blinding joy in the eyes of Perez, as though

45

he looked upon a bright treasure, in beholding Silver.

They swung their prisoner about. They began to sweep him down the roadway that led up to the house.

Behind them, Silver heard the girl saying: "A man who trusted you, brought you the news of the death, and the horse of Pedro for the proof! Uncle Arturo, what has come of the honor of the Montereys?"

"Where is there honor among the gringos?" thundered Monterey in answer. His voice swelled out enormously, from that withering body. "Do you speak to a Mexican of honor in dealing with them? Honor, in handling a brute who brings me the horse of my dead boy, and the word that *he* has killed him? Honor?"

The Mexicans had come to the horse of Silver, and now they flung him upon it. They had taken his guns, his knife. Some held the bridle of the horse; others gripped the legs, the arms of the prisoner. Still more were riding up horses from the patio, coming on the gallop. But the voice of the girl, like a meager hope of salvation and life, still found the ears of Silver, dimly, through the tumult.

She was saying: "He had faith in you. If you betray faith, God will never forgive you. What a man does innocently is not done at all. Uncle Arturo, you have only this moment to decide. They are taking him away—it will be too late—you will be shamed—and you will let in the law on us all. If you let him be killed, it is murder in the eyes of Heaven, and in the eyes of the law, also. Oh, if the ghost of Pedro is near us, it is giving an echo to what I say!"

But now the cavalcade had formed, half on horseback and half on foot, bearing Silver with them resistlessly, carrying him forward toward the quick ending of his life. He could see the big barrier of the mountains surging in steep-sided waves across the sky before him. His horse was shaking its head, and making the bridle ring. One of the Mexicans had a broad red stain on the shoulder of his white shirt. A wild jumble of detached observations came flooding into the brain of Silver. And through it, the voice of the girl, raised by desperation as distance made it fade.

Afterward, a dull cry reached them, calling Juan Perez. The man turned.

"She has persuaded him," said one of the escort. "Perez, what do you say? Shall we sweep him away? Aye, or kill him here in the roadway! Kill him here, and have it done?"

Perez, looking back up the road, saw something that made him fix on Silver the eye of a maniac. Then, with a gesture of despair, he halted the troop.

"Take him back!" he commanded. "The señor calls for him. The girl has won again. She always wins. We are only dogs to be barked back and forth. Perhaps this gringo fills her eyes; perhaps we shall have to lick his feet before long!"

The whole escort turned, gradually, and Silver could see again the stern old man standing as erect as ever, with his two hands resting on the head of his cane. The girl was beside him, withdrawn a little.

So they came straight back to confront Don Arturo. The passion was working in his face, still, and he was paler than before.

He cried out in that great voice which seemed to make his body smaller than ever, by contrast: "He has come to me, Juan Perez, and I must take thought before I put hands on him. But for his sake I shall forget the vow I made twenty-five years ago. He shall enter my house! He shall be taken into it now. Perez, carry him down to the cellar, to the lowest and the darkest room. There are irons to fit on him. Load him until his body is safely held. You, Perez, are his keeper, and shall answer to me for him!"

"Uncle Arturo—" cried out the girl.

"Be still—be still!" exclaimed the old man. "Do you talk to me of honor and kindness? They have shamed me, they have dishonored my house, they have ravaged my lands, and now they have slain my son, and leave me a dry, dead stalk! Juan Perez, do as I command!"

CHAPTER VIII

Imprisoned

THEY carried Silver rapidly into the house. The last he heard from the sunlit outdoors was the voice of the girl, raised higher than before as she passionately implored Don Arturo to remember himself, and the loud, stern cry of the old man as he bade her be quiet.

Out of a big corridor, they turned through a high and narrow doorway down a steep flight of steps. Lanterns were carried. Their swinging light began to flash far ahead, glimmering along damp walls, or throwing a dull sheen across the water that lay on the stones they trod, as they penetrated story after story, deep and deeper into the rock.

Juan Perez went first. Of the crowd, perhaps only half a dozen remained to hustle Silver along. And it seemed as though they were not descending through the cellars of a house, but through the galleries of some old mine, that had been worked for centuries, drill and pick and shovel digging into the living stone to find the treasure. It was a wilderness. Silver had attempted to keep track of the turns, the descents, the stairs, the sloping passages, but he gave it up. And three or four times even Juan Perez, who seemed to know the place well, came to a halt and swung his lantern from side to side before he made a choice between one gallery or another.

Once he stopped at a corridor hewn to a great size, and Juan Perez commented to his awed companions, that this was the place where the heart of the great lode had been found.

It was, in fact, through the galleries of an ancient mine that they were passing. But now they paused and took from a room a set of manacles brown with time. With these they went forward only a short distance until they came to another door, and opening this, the lantern light revealed a little room perhaps three steps by two in dimensions. On the irregular floor of it water had gathered, which had been scummed over with green; the air itself was very foul; and the odor of the slime was like a throttling hand on the throat.

There they fitted the irons to the body of Silver. Juan Perez, with a key, opened and locked them again. Then he stood back and lifted a lantern until the sheen of it fell upon the captive.

Half in dry stone and half in slime sat Silver, and met the eye of Juan Perez calmly. There was no word spoken. He heard only the softly inhaled breath of Perez, and saw the flash of his eyes and teeth as he grinned. Then the Mexicans left him. The door slammed shut with the booming noise of a cannon shot. And far away he heard the departing troop. They were laughing and shouting; even that laughter and derisive shouting seemed to Silver a precious thing to be harkened after with an eager ear. He strained his senses to hear every scruple of it; and when at last he could make out no more sound, the darkness was suddenly trebled about him, and a weight fell crushingly on his lungs.

It was the impure air that sickened him and made breathing almost futile. Presently he forgot the slime in which he lay, and, stretched flat on his back, did his best to calm the insane fear which was working in his brain.

Then began the first eternity, black, still, foul, breathless. He secured hope out of one strange thought—that he had appointed himself to redeem the lost life of Pedro Monterey, and that therefore he must suffer worse than

49

death, and then be given the chance to use his hands and his brain. He must nearly die, but some life would surely be left to him.

When we are in bed, clean, clear reason departs from us. And it departed, now, from Silver, as he lay in the stifling black of that prison. His second occupation was to employ his mind with dreams of what the life of Pedro Monterey must have been in this house with the stern old man for a father, and with all the fierce vaqueros ready to ride or to fight at his bidding. The girl, however, was not his sister. She was merely a cousin, more or less distant. And there was mercy in her which the pure strain of these Montereys seemed incapable of feeling.

She kept moving across the close velvet blackness that filled the eyes of Silver. She moved like a light before him, and filled his mind with a singular happiness.

Now, at the end of that eternity, there was the faint sound of footfalls. The lock of the door turned. A lantern flashed, blinding bright, throwing intolerable diamonds of brilliance into the eyes of Silver. By that light, dimly, he saw a jug put down beside the door, and a lump of bread was thrown toward him. It splashed in the slimy water. A voice laughed, and the door shut heavily again.

But he found himself forgetful of the spoiling of the bread, and of the contents of the jug, though he was starving for food, and famished for water. All that he bent his attention on was the noise of the retreating footfalls.

When it had dissolved, still a faint echo worked in his brain, as though to reassure him that there were human beings left in the world. Then he started toward the door, dragging his body along with great difficulty. He found the jug and sniffed at it. He had hoped for something better than water, but when he lifted the pitcher with his manacled hands, it was water alone that he tasted. Yet it flooded his hot throat with wonderful relief.

When he had drunk, hunger returned to him with new force. He had seen the bread fall into the rotten slime, but revolting as the sight had been, he sought for that bread now, and found it, and tried to eat it, but the repulsive taste made the walls of his stomach close together in nausea.

He threw the food from him and stretched himself again to wait.

The cold of the stone was sinking into his body, reaching the bone. He knew that weakness caused by lack of food was making him more and more susceptible to the cold. He must use his muscles to gain heat from them, no matter how the efforts increased his hunger. So he devised a regular system, getting painfully to his feet, bowing, forward and backward, swaying to the side, stretching his loaded arms as far as the chains permitted, then squatting and rising, squatting and rising until he was numb with the efforts.

Those exercises kept his blood coursing in the veins. And afterward it was easier to sleep. But sleep occupied only a small portion of the second infinity of darkness before he saw more light. When he wakened, there was a new, pungent, horrible odor in the air, a sort of sickening sweetness, and a moment later he heard the pattering of infinitely light feet, the squeak and gibbering of sharp voices.

Rats were in the room with him!

He felt a sudden blind horror, a horror of squeamishness. He actually parted his lips to scream out; but the man in him came to his rescue and sternly throttled back that weakness. Yet what would he be in the course of a few weeks or months? But were there not men who had lain for long years in darkness, like beasts, and still endured?

Hope came to him with the rats. If they had entered, it was by some hole, and if there were a small hole, he might enlarge it. He began to work with his finger tips across the entire surface of the wall, knowing that touch would give to him the effect of sight, in a sense.

What he found, at last, was a narrow crevice, so small that it seemed impossible that even a mouse could have come through. But it was not in masonry that might be crumbled gradually away from this small start; it was a rift in the living stone, strong as iron on either side of the little aperture.

He gave up that hope slowly, and his spirits and his strength seemed to ebb away from him for a long time afterward.

He went through the exercises again, as he had devised them. And now he sat in a dry corner and waited.

At last the steps came again, the door opened, and again a light shone on him. The lantern was raised high;

he saw the face of the girl beneath it, as she saw him.

"Phaugh!" she cried. "Rats, and slime, and filth for a Christian man. In the name of mercy, Juan Perez, what—"

The voice of Perez answered sullenly: "Any sort of life is too good for him. The rats keep him company. Some day I hope they'll eat him!"

She stepped in, and pushed the door shut behind her. And her coming poured upon Silver wave after wave of incredible comfort and joy. He had hardly thought her more than pretty in the sunlight; in the dark, damp room she seemed to have the radiant beauty of an angel.

Perez was calling out, beyond the door. She silenced him with two or three sharp words of command. Then she came closer, picking her way between the puddles of slime. Silver struggled, and rose to his feet with a clanking of chains.

He towered above her, and she with a lifted face looked at him with pity and with pain.

"Have they given you food?" she asked.

"They threw one lump of bread—into the slime," he said. "They knew I could not eat it, after that."

"No food, then? Three days without food?" she cried. "Three days?"

"Three years, it seems to me," said Silver, "of this darkness."

She hurried to the door and pulled the weight of it open.

"Perez," she gasped, her voice shaking with anger. "Quickly! Run to the kitchen. Bring meat—a good meal—a huge meal—and wine—and bring it with your own hands—quickly!"

Juan Perez snarled like a dog, but his footfall departed.

CHAPTER IX

Señorita Julia

SHE came slowly back, a step or two, and then paused. "They have treated you like a dog," she said, "and I knew when I first saw you, that you are an honest man. You're weak. Sit down and—Great heavens, you've nothing to sit on but the damp of the stone! Phaugh! The rats want to come back!"

They had scampered through the crevice in the wall, as she entered with the light, their naked tails flicking like whiplashes out of view. Now their eyes glittered from the mouth of the covert again.

"God forgive Uncle Arturo," she said. And then she broke out: "Yet there's no kinder or more gentle man in the world. But his son is dead, and his hope is dead, too, and he's half insane with grief. He had to put his hands on something, and there were you in his grasp! And then Drummons—what's left to him now for the fight with them? Only his own hands, and mine, and only half my blood is that of the Montereys! You can understand him a little, and forgive him a little?"

He said nothing.

"I came to ask you one definite thing," she said, when

she saw that he would not speak on the other subject. "What was in your mind when you came to this house to tell us that you had killed poor Pedro?"

"Have they sent for his body? Will he be buried here?" asked Silver.

"They have sent for him," she answered.

"When I saw by the flash of my own gun that I had shot the wrong man," said Silver, "I don't think I would have cared so much if he had been older. But he was at the start of everything. He hadn't had a chance to prove himself. And—well, it's a hard thing to talk about. I really can't tell you what I thought."

He ended abruptly, but she was watching him with such studious and yet such gentle eyes that presently his words began again, as if of their own accord.

"I thought," said Silver, "that I could try to fill in some of the gap left by his death. I was a fool. I couldn't tell that he was the only son of this old man. I thought that I could do something about him. And somehow," he added, his voice swelling as the old resolution burned back into his brain hotter than ever, and more inwardly bright, "and somehow, I think I'll manage to put my hands on something that he left unfinished, and complete it for him. I suppose this sounds like crazy talk to you. And I won't beat about the bush. I've killed other men—more than one or two! But this time it was different. To kill a man is bad enough; but to finish a life that's hardly begun to cut its own way through the world—that was what made me sick, then! And—"

He paused, with a gesture. He felt that he had talked absolutely in vain.

She merely said: "I believe you, and I understand you. And for that bigness of heart, you've been thrown into this blackness and treated like a murderer! Ah, but my uncle shall hear about it from me! I'll make him understand!"

Then, turning, she exclaimed: "Here's Juan Perez back again. You shall eat, now!"

The door was pushed open, and it was Juan Perez indeed. He carried a small half loaf of bread in one hand and a jug of water in the other. He put down the jug, laid the bread across the mouth of it, and then straightened to face the girl with a grin.

That smile made him look more like a hungry tiger than ever.

"Señorita Julia," he said, "the señor forbids the prisoner to have more than bread and water."

"You went to him?" exclaimed the girl. "You went to him, after I had given you my orders?"

"We serve you, señorita," said the politely sneering Perez, "as we would serve an angel. But there is only one master in the house of Monterey!"

He made a little bow to her, and lifting his head again, he stared not at her but at Silver, with unabated hatred.

The girl was instantly calm.

"I shall see my uncle," said she. "And some changes will be made. You shall have a bed. I think I can make him change your room. Perhaps there will be decent food, after a little while."

She went to the door and turned suddenly. Her eyes flashed. Her voice flared up. Color burned into her face.

"Day and night," she exclaimed, "I shall try to serve you, señor!"

She was gone. Perez, lantern in hand, looked after her, toward the door, and then shook his forefinger in the air. He began to laugh, in a silent convulsion of mirth.

"Those words will undo everything else she may say to the master," he told Silver. "Day and night she will serve you, gringo. Is that the truth? Señor Monterey shall hear what she said. I shall see to that. And afterward—hai! You'll feel the spur as well as the toe of the boot!"

He laughed again, this time out loud, and left Silver in the black darkness.

And there Silver crouched, chewing eagerly at the bread, while the rats swarmed over his feet, leaped up on his clothes, in their eagerness to come at the food. The air was foul with the smell of their vile bodies, but the ravenous hunger of Silver stilled all the other senses. He ate, drank the water to the last drop, and then lay down and slept. Something would be done for him. The girl had promised. And he would believe her more than the oaths of a hundred men.

But nothing was done!

Bread and water were brought to him regularly, once a day, and that was all. The cell was not changed. Not one item of comfort was added to him. And two days later, Juan Perez came again, alone. He unlocked the door, put the lantern on the floor, and made a cornucopia-shaped cigarette, which he lighted, and then blew the smoke toward Silver, to make sure that the full flavor of the tobacco would reach him. The very heart of Silver quaked with yearning, but he made his eye calm, and kept it fixed on the Mexican.

"So I repeated the kind words of the Señorita Julia to the master," said Juan Perez. "And you see what has happened? You see the comfortable bed you lie on? You see the warm sunshine that streams through your window? You taste the good tobacco that is given you to smoke? You breathe the pure air? You relish the fine roasts and the stews and the dried meats that are brought to you? For all of those things, Señor Fool, Señor Dog, you can thank Juan Perez!"

Silver slowly dragged up his legs until they were half doubled under him. A plan was forming dimly in his brain. Now he merely smiled at Perez. That smile seemed to strike the Mexican like a blow. He started, and then scowled.

"You think that you've tormented me, Perez," said Silver. "As a matter of fact, I have to stay here for another day or two. That is all. Then I shall leave. Before I go, I shall have certain words to say to you, certain blows to strike you with a whip, certain speeches that I shall listen to you making on your knees, while you grovel before me, and beg for your life."

"Dog!" breathed Juan Perez. "You mean that I, Perez, shall be on my knees before you? You mean that in a day or two you'll be gone? Ah, I see—your mind is touched, you are losing your wits in the long darkness!"

"Poor Perez!" said Silver. "You cannot understand?"

"Understand?" said the Mexican, coming a stride closer. "What is there to understand?"

"That you have been a fool from the first! You can't understand that?" said Silver.

"I? I a fool? I who walk with free feet and eat and sleep as I will, and breathe the fresh air—I am the fool—and you are the wise man?"

He drew a shade closer.

Silver leaned his head and shoulders back against the wall. And he smiled at Juan Perez as if out of the deeps of a profound contentment.

"Poor Juan Perez!" he said, and shook his head a little, as though words could not fit the matter.

"Gringo beast!" gasped Perez suddenly, and striding one step nearer, he struck Silver full in the face.

The next instant the legs of the Mexican were knocked from under him, for the two manacled feet of Silver had shot out with a true aim and a desperate vigor. Perez, falling, pitched straight forward at the prisoner. Silver, with both hands raised, met the dropping body with a club stroke over the head. The weight of the irons on his wrists helped home that blow, and Juan Perez lay face down on the stones, without a quiver.

Silver went through the man's pockets. He knew, he thought, the very look and face of the key that fitted into his manacles. And he found it in the pocket of the deerskin vest of Perez. It was clumsy work to fit that key into the lock of the hand irons, and it was impossible to turn it with his fingers. He had to go to the little crevice in the wall, and there laboriously fit the handle of the key into the base of the crack, and then turn his arms until the lock was sprung. But a moment later he was free, both in arms and hands and feet.

A wave of half hysterical delight shot through him, and centered in his throat.

It was dashed away, a moment later, by the fear that he heard footfalls hurrying down the corridor outside his room. Then he realized that it was merely the beat and flutter of his racing heart.

Juan Perez groaned, and sat up. He saw Silver standing over him, with the gun of Perez himself in his hand, and he groaned. In the rage of his despair, he cast himself back, and the slime into which he fell was flung out in a fine spray on either side.

"You see, Perez?" said Silver. "After all, you were a fool, and sooner than you expected. But be patient, my friend. When you leave this room, a good many things may have happened, and, above all, the whole world will know that Perez is a fool!"

He took the lantern, and left the Mexican groaning,

beating his head with his hands. He left the room. A small, cold draft was stirring in the corridor, and as Silver locked the heavy door behind him, and pocketed the key, it seemed to him that all the freshness of the spring and the sweetness of spring flowers was in that air!

He went up the hallway. There was no plan in his mind. He must simply pray that it was night, that he could be able to reach the outer door that led into the patio, that he could pass from the patio into freedom.

And leave behind him the great task unfinished, and poor Pedro Monterey doubly dead?

His heart failed him, when he thought of making such a surrender. Have not men said that nothing is impossible to the resolute mind? He thought of that saying, also, as he roamed up the corridors beneath the house of Monterey. But it seemed to him that it would be almost a sufficient miracle if he could save his life from the hands of the old man.

But the thing persisted in him. He had set his soul on the purpose for too long. And the completion of the life of Pedro Monterey had become a spiritual necessity to him. That was why, as he roved through the passages, he began to deny in himself the thought of mere flight and take to his heart a greater steadiness.

If he were to remain near Monterey, another miracle must happen, greater than any which had gone before. But Silver determined to let the events of each moment dictate what he was to do with himself in the immediate future.

There was the problem of getting up from the cellars at all. And that seemed enough to fill his mind. For hours he wandered, and always he was coming to the end of passages that stopped against solid stone. The flame in the lantern burned low, flickered, died. He was left in a horror of darkness that seemed to keep flowing past him.

A man might pass days, fumbling through that blindness, and never come to an exit. He might be so far lost that not even the faintest echo of his voice would reach to any ears.

Silver leaned against a wall and closed his eyes, and tried to find in his mind some solution, but all his thoughts were whirling, spinning like foolish squirrels in a cage.

He was still standing there when something clinked like

the lock of a door. He looked up, and a flash of light entered the passage just before him, and footfalls came clumping down steps. Then light shone again, swinging out from behind the voluminous skirts of a woman.

Silver crouched close to the floor, with hope once more in his heart. The light disappeared. The woman was singing softly as she went on some familiar errand, her wooden heels bumping on the stone.

But what was important to Silver was that door through which she had come, for it seemed that his lantern had failed him when he was very few steps from salvation.

He hurried through the darkness, spreading his hands far out before him. Then his feet struck the steps. He climbed. He came, at the top of the steps, to the kind touch of wood, and fumbling, he soon found the knob.

Softly he opened the door, and peered out. At once the rattle of many voices in laughter and raillery struck on his ears as if with open mockery of all that he was attempting.

CHAPTER X

In the Garden

HE SHRANK back, then thrust the door wide in a sudden desperation. And springing out into the hall, he discovered to his amazement that it was empty.

Still the voices persisted, but plainly they must come from some adjoining room, beating through a thin partition.

He went rapidly to the end of the hall. The clinking of his spurs followed him like an accusing voice, so he drew off his boots, and left them in a corner.

He tried the nearest door. It opened with a dull groan of hinges and let him into a big room. He knew its bigness, only, by the faintest of high lights that glimmered here and there in the chamber. It was a bedroom, and crossing it to the stars that filled a window, he looked out and down.

Beneath him, he saw still another drop of twenty feet of unbroken wall, with a garden spread over the ground under the window. He must be on the first floor of the house, but on this side another story was added below. It was just the garden that a Mexican would conceive in happy dreams—a little flat of ground with a canal of water lilies driven through it, and a rectangular pool at one end, with a fountain rising over it. That was the chief feature, together with a semicupola, a sort of open-faced summer-house raised on narrow columns, so that one would have both shade and wind.

Silvertip saw this by the light of a big yellow moon which was lifting over the eastern mountains with its cheeks still puffed beyond the full. And this light showed him, moreover, a table laid in the cool beside the canal of water lilies. The girl, Julia, sat there, and opposite her old Monterey, rigid with dignity. The moon gleamed faintly on his long hair and his pointed beard.

There was no escape by that window. So Silvertip turned, and, crouching low so that no light might strike up and outward through the window, he scratched a match. Cupping the flame securely in his hands, he threw the dull flash of it here and there about the room. He saw, at once, a small door to the right; he saw the big bed, like a mahogany house, the fireplace, and above it a portrait that drew him suddenly across the room. He ventured rising and passing the light from the match across the face in the picture. It was Pedro Monterey, younger, and alive and smiling.

The flame of the match seared the fingers of Silvertip before he dropped it on the hearth, and still in the darkness he remained staring before him as though he could still see the portrait. The bitterness he had been feeling toward old Monterey now vanished. It was only strange to him that the slayer of the son had not been slain out of hand.

He fumbled his way with outstretched hands through the darkness and came to the little door that he had seen on the right. When he opened it, a cool breath of air moved upward into his face. And he had a sense, though no sight, of steps descending through the shadows before him. With his foot he reached and found, as he had expected, a stairway that led down. He shut the door behind him. The draft no longer blew. A close dampness of moist stone surrounded him as he descended a winding way until one outstretched hand told him of another door.

He opened it with great care, and instantly found the outdoors before his face, the yellow of the moonlight

61

striking directly against him. It was the garden where the girl sat with Monterey.

The silhouette of a man moved before him, close enough to touch. But the figure did not pause at the partially opened door. It went on, bearing a large tray with glasses twinkling on it, and a luster of half-seen silver.

Silvertip ventured outside. Other people moved here and there, but all at a sufficiently safe distance, so he stole for the nearest shelter. It was a bank of shadow that looked to him like brush, but turned out to be tall flowers, which were hedged up here as a margin and border to surround the garden.

Delicately he moved forward, putting the great, rank stalks aside until he had made for himself a covert of darkness. There he crouched, and parting the branches before him, he could look out on the garden scene and the table with a more intimate eye.

They spoke suddenly, and then turned their faces directly toward him.

"There is something in the flowers," said the girl.

"There is the wind," said the voice of Señor Monterey.

"Something moved in there, slowly," she insisted.

"A snake, perhaps," suggested the old man.

He dismissed the subject with a wave of his hand. The wind stirred his long hair, and his beard, and the moon glittered over him till he looked to Silvertip like a patriarchal form that had walked out of a distant age.

"You think of him still," said Monterey suddenly.

The bowed head of the girl lifted slowly. And a touch on the heart of Silver told him that it was of him that Monterey was speaking. That was hardly strange.

"I think of him," she answered. "I keep thinking. I keep trying for words that will move you, Uncle Arturo."

The old man answered: "You would not need to whisper to me, Julia, if I dreamed that he is what you say— honest! But he can't be honest. There is no honesty in his race. I have suffered at their hands enough to have broken the hearts of twenty stronger men than I, and only my hope for revenge keeps life in me. Now that my boy is gone, you will wonder that I can still hope even for revenge, but let me tell you that the dream has been in my heart so long that it cannot die as quickly as Pedrillo did.

I think that even bullets could not kill it. If my body came to an end, the hate for the gringos would still live. It would take a bodiless form; it would walk the earth like a ghost. But no matter how I hate his race, if this man were honest, I would set him free, reward him, beg for his pardon."

"He is honest, if I ever saw honesty!" said the girl. "And now he lies in a pen where you would not even put swine!"

"He is like his people—a liar and a traitor!" exclaimed Monterey. "How many times they have betrayed me, Julia! You know only a little of it! And now I think of how he tried to deceive you, of how he told you that he came here only hoping that he could fill the place of my dead boy, in some way. Oh, my child, it was the sort of a story that a man might use to a woman, but never to another man."

"Uncle Arturo," said the girl, "he came with the horse, he told the truth of the death of poor Pedro, and he put himself in your hands. How could he have done those things unless he meant honestly?"

But there was no response to her plea. After a pause of silence, the girl stirred.

"To the good, all creatures are virtuous," said Monterey, "and there is such a well of goodness in you that you could forgive the devil himself for his craft and his fiendishness. You would pity him for the pain that he lies in. But let me tell you that I shall never again believe well of a gringo until his virtue is established more plainly than the mountains that stand by the Haverhill Valley!"

She looked steadily at the old man for a moment. Then she sighed.

"It's time to go in," said Julia. "Oñate and Alvarez have been quarreling again, and you'll have to see them."

"I can see them out here," said Arturo Monterey.

"It's not safe," she answered. She leaned a little across the table. "The men of Drummon are bolder every day; how can you tell how bold they'll be at night? They may slip up here. They have a moon to show them their way. They may be here now. What I heard there among the flowers may be one of them lying still and watching, and listening."

"Let them watch, and let them listen," said Monterey.

"I have a feeling, Julia, that I've come to the end of my day. Let it close as soon as it will. I'm ready for it."

The girl waited an instant. Then she said: "You're tired to-day, Uncle Arturo. And when a person is tired, the gloomy thoughts are the ones that come up in the mind."

He answered: "I've been marked by my shame long enough, and if I am to die, I am ready for it."

He touched his forehead significantly as he spoke, on the band of dark cloth that crossed his forehead.

The girl would have spoken again, but he stopped her with a raised hand, saying:

"There is nothing but cold and emptiness in my heart. And I should die even gladly, except that there is the one great purpose of all these years unaccomplished."

"But if you stay out here," said the girl, "if you throw yourself away into the hands of Drummon's brutes—is there any chance, then, of doing what you promised yourself?"

He answered: "If the hand of God is against me, why should I attempt to defend myself?"

CHAPTER XI

Brand of Shame

OLD Monterey was asking to have Oñate and Alvarez brought before him. They must have been attending close at hand, for now they came in, together, escorted by two vaqueros who had bound the hands of the pair. And they stood with bowed heads before the master. One was young, one a grizzled veteran. They were peons of the field, not cattle herders; they wore *huarachos* on their bare feet, and they were dressed in white cotton that shimmered in the moonlight.

"Now, Tonio?" said Arturo Monterey.

One of the vaqueros made half a step forward. He was a solid fellow with a grave, steady look.

"Their houses are side by side, as you know, señor," said Tonio. "They have always been friends. Oñate is a good man, and he has helped Alvarez. He's older, this Oñate, and he has a head on his shoulders. But now, all at once, they are enemies. They run at each other with knives. We ask them why they quarrel. They give us no answer. They will not speak to each other. They will not speak to us. So we have brought them to you, señor."

"Who began this quarrel?" asked Monterey.

The two peons looked at one another, and were silent, staring again at the ground.

"Answer!" cried Monterey, lifting his voice suddenly to thunder.

They both started violently, and with one voice, both exclaimed: "I started the trouble, señor."

Then they were mute, and again gaped on one another.

"You both began the fight?" said Monterey, amused and interested. "How could you both begin it?"

"It was I, señor," said Oñate. "I am sorry, and I repent."

"I am sorry, and I repent, also," said Alvarez. Then, losing his control for an instant, he exclaimed: "But this Oñate is a liar and a fool!"

Oñate, grinding his teeth, said nothing. He continued to look merely at the ground.

"You both began the fight; you both repent; and one of you is a liar and a fool. How, Oñate? Are you the liar and the fool?"

Oñate jerked up his head savagely. Then something from within gave him pause. He drew a breath and gasped, "Yes, señor."

Monterey regarded them both soberly.

"They have seen you; perhaps it is enough. They will not fight again, señor," observed Tonio.

Monterey hushed him with a gesture.

"Fire can burn underground, but it will always break out when a wind blows," he said. "Why did you quarrel, you two?"

Again the pair regarded one another, gloomily.

"Speak!" commanded Monterey.

Oñate said slowly: "I, señor, said a foolish thing. I am sorry. I angered Alvarez. I ask him to forgive me. I am —a liar—a fool!"

He brought out the last words with a bitter effort.

"There is no more lying in you, Oñate, than in a blessed saint," declared Monterey. "What was it you talked about?"

There was another pause, but not so long that Monterey had to lay the whip of his impatience on either of them again. For Alvarez muttered:

"About you, señor, and God forgive us!"

"God will forgive you and so shall I, probably," said Monterey. "What was it that you said about me?"

This time the full pause lasted so long, before an answer, that the silence itself became more of a threat than any words from Monterey could have been. It was this quiet pressure that made Alvarez say:

"I asked Oñate if he knew why the señor wore the cloth band about his head, always, day and night. And then he told me such a great lie that my knife got into my hand. But even a good man will lie, sometimes, to make talk. I am sorry. But the señor is my father; he is the father to us all."

Monterey was so moved by something in this speech that he stood up from his chair, suddenly.

"What did you say, Oñate?" he demanded.

"Señor," he said, "if you ask me for my words, I shall seem to you a traitor and a scoundrel. In the name of Heaven, do not make me speak, and forgive me!"

Monterey bowed his head for a moment in thought.

"The time has come, Oñate," he said, "when secret shame should be bared before the world. My son has gone from me, Oñate, and I fear that he will not return. Perhaps the secrecy with which I have kept that shame of mine is the reason that God chooses to punish me. Speak out, freely. What did you say to Alvarez?"

Oñate flung himself suddenly on his knees.

"Señor," he groaned, "it is a foul story that has been in the air for many years, since the night when Señor Drummon and his men poured into the house. And it is said— forgive me for repeating it!—but it is said that on that night the brand of the Cross and Snake was burned into your forehead with your own branding iron by the gringo devils!"

He put up a hand before his face, as though to shield himself from an unexpected blow.

The girl sprang up and hurried to the side of Arturo Monterey, anxiously, as though to be a shield to any object of his wrath. But the old man, after a moment, cried out:

"It is the will of God that the whole world should know. Oñate, you spoke the truth."

With that, he suddenly tore the cloth band from about

his head, and the brightness of the moon showed to them all, and above all to the straining eyes of Silvertip, a small cross printed in a shadowy furrow in the brow of Monterey, and beneath it a wavering line—the complete brand of the Cross and Snake.

The Mexicans, both the prisoners and the vaqueros who had guarded them, slowly drew back from that sight, then turned, and fairly fled. Monterey slipped back into his chair and the girl, lifting the cloth circle from the ground, fitted it carefully over the bowed head again. She was weeping, stifling her sobs as well as she could. Then she sat beside him, watching his bowed face.

"The whole world had heard of it," said Monterey. "You have heard of it also, Julia. Drummon has talked of it and boasted of it among his men. That is why the gringos laugh, when they look at me, and laugh, also, when they speak of me."

"The cruel, savage dogs!" sobbed the girl. "I had heard of it, Uncle Arturo, but I would never believe. None of us would ever believe. Why did you show it to them?"

"The will of God," repeated Monterey. "Who can avoid that? And yet perhaps, before the end, I shall be able to strike one blow at Drummon. I have prayed for that. I have yearned for it, since that night when Drummon and his men broke into this house and lashed me to a chair in my own hall, and heated the branding iron in the coals of my own fire."

"No!" cried the girl. "No one could do that to you! Not even a beast like Drummon, or the brutes that follow him!"

"He told me," said Monterey, "that since I fought with him about the cattle in the valley, and since I claimed more than was mine, he would put my own brand where the devil himself and every man could always see it. And then he took the branding iron with his own hands. It was white-hot. It threw out snapping sparks, and the heat seemed to drip away in shining water. He stamped the brand in the middle of the forehead, and burned the flesh through, to the bone. Then he left me, and I heard their laughter go like a roaring wind through the house. He left me with the brand on my forehead, and a ruined right hand, so that I could never strike back."

He lifted that hand, and Silvertip saw for the first time that it was a withered, twisted, inturned claw.

"Do you wonder, Julia," said Monterey, "that I raised Pedrillo to be a warrior, and that I taught him very little besides riding and shooting with rifles and revolvers? Do you wonder that I brought in the gun fighter and man-killer, José Bandini, to be a tutor to him, at last? For I had sworn that when he reached his twenty-first year, he should have to leave my house, and never return to it unless he had fulfilled my promise to Drummon. I swore to him, Julia, as he stood back from me—I swore to Drummon, when the pain had blinded me, that I would do to him as he had done to me, but more, and lay this brand of mine on the door of his house, on his forehead, and over his heart. Do you understand why I have waited these years? I married in hope of having a son; when he was born, I gave my life to raising him for that one purpose. And he is gone, Julia. He has been swept away. So I remain alone, with only this to perform my task!"

And he lifted, again, the withered right hand which was his only tool for labor.

CHAPTER XII

Drummon's Men

It HAD come to Silvertip like a thunderstroke of revelation. The sense of folly and of wasted effort departed from him; the whole cloud of obscurity was not lifted, but he could see his major purpose emerge clear and straight before him. He knew to what end the life of Pedrillo Monterey had been aimed; now he had before him, clearly, the definite goal. On the door of the Drummon house, on Drummon's brow, and over his heart to place the brand which had been stamped so brutally into the forehead of Monterey—that was to be the task. The joy that swelled suddenly in the heart of Silvertip could not be contained by the cold constriction of fear that also gathered about it.

And as the bewilderment left him, as the purpose became clear before him, he was struck again with wonder as to how he should be able to approach Monterey, to offer his services. His face was known in the house—and the Mexicans were prepared to hunt him like a beast.

He heard the girl saying: "We must go in, Uncle Arturo. It's growing very cool, now. And it's late."

"It's late," said Monterey, "and it's too cool for you

70

out here now. But I want to be alone, Julia. I have to be alone for a time. Go in, my dear, and I'll stay out here for a few moments."

"Then let me call some of the men," said the girl.

"So that they can guard me under the wall of my own house?" asked Monterey angrily. "So that they can stare at me, and whisper to each other because of the shame they've seen stamped on my face forever, this evening? No, I'll stay here alone. And if Drummon's hunting wolves come near enough to nip me, they will not be taking a great prize. Go in, Julia."

She lingered for a moment, then, as though persuaded by some inward impulse, she left him silently, and passed into the house.

Arturo Monterey, when she had gone, walked to each side of the terrace, and peered across the hollow of the valley. Then he returned and sat at the table, staring north. A gust of wind, iced from the mountain snows, struck coldly across the garden, making the tall perennials around Silvertip whip up and down with a rushing sound.

The breeze fell away, and old Monterey remained at his place unmoved by the cold, lost in his thoughts. Again the wind fanned his silver hair, ruffling and raising it, sending through the flowers rustlings that seemed to continue even after all the breeze had died.

It was time, Silver knew, to step out and confront the Mexican. Sooner or later he had to face him and make his offer, in whatever words he could find. But still he delayed. One shout from Monterey would bring men pouring out from the house; and perhaps the shout would come before he could explain himself.

So he waited, irresolute, and now heard the rustling among the tall flowers again, though it seemed to him that there was no wind at all. Something pulled his glance suddenly up, and he saw two figures rise almost beside him. The back of Monterey was turned toward them; it did not need a glimpse of the shotgun one carried or of the revolver that shimmered in the hand of the other to tell Silvertip that these were the men of Drummon. They were black against the sky, their faces darkened under the wide brims of their sombreros as though they had been rubbed with charcoal.

Silvertip's Colt was in his grip as he rose, shouting: "Monterey!"

The old man leaped up; a revolver spat twice. To Silvertip the gun seemed to make hardly a sound; he was more aware of the shotgun, which was being swung toward him; and at that fellow he fired.

The man dropped his weapon. He ran stumbling forward, stretching out his arms before him as one who has lost balance. Right between Silvertip and the second of Drummon's men he ran, and lurched into the flowers at Silver's feet with a crash. Silvertip was already firing over him, as the body fell, but the second stalker had taken to flight and ran like a snipe flying down wind.

Already he was through the opposite border of flowers, and racing down the slope beyond. Silver, running in pursuit, saw old Monterey standing by the table with a small pocket pistol raised to an attitude of attention, like a duelist in another day, waiting for the word to fire.

When Silvertip gained the edge of the terrace, he saw his quarry already in a cluster of tall shrubbery, out of which the fugitive sped away on a horse. There was no purpose in pursuit. The moon flashed for an instant on the striding of the mustang; then it was lost among great trees, like a hawk in a dark cloud.

Silvertip whirled back, to find that Monterey already was kneeling beside the fallen body, trying to turn it over. That task Silvertip performed for him, and as a door of the house crashed open, as wild voices poured out at them, Silver turned on its back the powerful body and the wide, brutal face of Chuck Terry.

His mind flashed back to the picture of young Pedrillo Monterey, lying smiling at the ceiling, and Silver felt that at last he had made one long stride down the trail on which he had set his foot.

They were all around him now, Tonio and the girl among the first, with others filling in the background. Every man of them was armed. They would have pulled down Silvertip like a pack of hungry dogs, if the voice of Monterey had not stopped them.

"That is the gringo who brought the mare, señor!" shouted some one.

"By the grace of God!" said Monterey. "Otherwise I

should have lain where this one is lying. He has saved me, my children. He has killed this murderer, and made another run like a deer. Do you know the face of the dead man, any one of you?"

They came up to look at that immobile face, and as they passed by Silvertip, they looked with fear, with wonder, with hatred, also, upon him. He felt the shifting of their eyes upward, to the two gray tufts of his hair, like incipient horns rising. Tonio made the sign against the evil eye.

"This one is called Terry," said Tonio. "He is one of the leaders for Drummon. He is one who hires others. We have seen him before come near the house, like a buzzard sailing in a clear sky. And now he's caught and down—caught and down! Gringo! Hai! You grin at us now, eh? But we are laughing. If all—"

"Be quiet, Tonio," said Monterey. "Do you forget that this man who has saved my life is also an American?"

He went up to Silver and faced him closely. All of Monterey's visage was old, the lines down-flowing from the brows and the mouth, but the eyes remained unflattened and undimmed by years, like the eyes of an artist.

"Take the body away," said Monterey to the peons. "And leave me alone with this man."

He remained standing close to Silver. The girl had come up beside him. And the servants rapidly picked up and carried away the dead man. One of his arms hung down, and the loose, dead fingers trailed along the ground.

"Sit down," said Monterey suddenly. "Sit here. You are weak. Julia, pour some wine. Here, señor. Sit down!"

He made Silver take the very chair in which he had been seated. He took the glass of wine from Julia, and passed it to Silver.

"I cannot drink alone!" said Silver.

"You shall not," said Arturo Monterey, and put a little wine in two more glasses.

The old man held up one of them as high as his head, until the wine sparkled in the moonlight.

"I see you in clothes covered with the slime of the cellar water," said Monterey. "I see you with a haggard and unshaven face, señor, and for every hair that grows upon it, I know you have had a bitter thought about me. How

I wish, now, that I could have seen you with the clear eyes of Julia! But I can only drink to you now out of the gratitude of my heart. Gratitude, señor, to the man who killed my—"

The words disappeared in a groan.

"I ask your forgiveness," went on Monterey, suddenly, as Silver rose from the chair. "I drink to kindliness between us, and perfect trust!"

"To the trust between us!" said Silver, and drank the wine. And over the edge of the glass his eyes found the eyes of old Monterey, and held them.

They lowered the glasses, all three.

"Were you here when I spoke to Julia of the past?" asked Monterey.

"I was here," said Silver.

"You have seen the Drummons," said Monterey, "and everything that I said about them is less than the truth. One of them you have killed. Therefore the whole tribe will hunt you down. You must leave the valley. You shall have guides and fast horses. Once beyond the mountains, you will be safe. In five minutes you must leave!"

"Not unless you gather your men and have me tied into a saddle and make them lead me out," answered Silver.

"Do you hear?" said the girl softly. "Uncle Arturo, do you hear? He will not leave you!"

"He *must* leave me," answered Monterey. "He has been treated like a dog. There must still be hatred in him."

"The wine has washed it away," answered Silver. "Señor, I am bound to this valley by an oath."

"To whom?" asked Monterey.

"To a dead man," said Silver. "It is a promise I made to Pedro Monterey as he lay dead. I swore then that I would never give up his back trail until I found what purpose he had in life, and that I would try to fulfill it. Tonight I've heard of the thing he was to do. I shall stay here in the Haverhill until there is the Cross and Snake brand on the door of the Drummon house, on the forehead of Drummon, and over his heart."

The words were somewhat magniloquent; the voice that spoke them was perfectly quiet and subdued. Arturo Monterey stared at the speaker, and then at the girl.

"I understand," he said at last. "And now that you have

spoken, there is no word fit to make a reply to you. You have spoken to Juan Perez. Even Perez could believe you, and that is why you were free to come here?"

Silver smiled faintly.

"Perez is lying in the room where I was kept," he answered. "He came to see me. I managed to knock his feet from under him, stun him, get the key, and free myself. After that I locked the door on him, and it was mostly chance that brought me here."

"Chance?" cried Monterey. "Chance? There is no chance in it! If ever God showed His hand, it is in this."

Monterey turned to the girl.

"Do you hear, Julia?" he asked.

"I hear," she said, watching the face of Silver all the while.

The old man lifted his voice, suddenly and loudly: "I believe! Do you see a justice in this? The very people who wronged me have sent me a champion. Providence is working. In every way, this surpasses ordinary human accident. The man is sent to me as a helper; he is attacked in front of my house; he is imprisoned; he breaks out to save my life, and offers me his own good right hand to help me in the fight. Do you see, Julia? It is a stroke out of the sky!"

He lifted his hand over his head as he spoke, and Silvertip saw the grisly distortion of it, a black, twisted thing against the brilliance of the moonlit sky. The voice and the hand of old Monterey fell at one moment. The strength dissolved out of him. He took the arm of the girl on one side and the arm of the gringo on the other, and so went slowly into the house.

CHAPTER XIII

Accepted

MONTEREY himself led the way to a closed door and paused before it. He said to Silvertip: "When a man comes closer to the grave, he comes nearer to a belief in many things formerly deemed incredible. I am old, my friend, and therefore I am superstitious. I take you as a great gift out of the hand of fortune. Señor Silver, for twenty-five years nobody of your race has entered this house, but now I am opening a room for you. I open this door for you, I open my hand and my heart and my faith to you, also."

He cast the door open. A servant carried in a lighted lamp before them to reveal a big chamber. Silvertip saw a gleaming of dark, polished wooden chests of drawers and a huge wardrobe, and the slender, shining posts of another big four-poster bed. The servant pushed open the heavy shutters of two windows and let the thin dappling of the stars be seen. They looked both close and dim, except one burning yellow eye of light.

Old Monterey took Silver's hand.

"In everything you say and everything you do,"

he said, "you are now as the master of the house. Señor, good night. An old man gives you his blessing."

The girl went out with him. The servant remained for a moment, moving slowly here and there to open the bed, to dust the window sills, which were covered with fine silt. Before he left, the fellow paused at the door and looked at Silvertip out of narrowed eyes. He continued to stare, unwinking, for a moment, then he nodded, and, with a muttered good night, left the room.

Silver could not settle down at once. He had to walk between the hall door and the windows, back and forth, back and forth, struggling with the thoughts that worked like moles under the surface of his mind.

As he looked back on the events that had occurred since that evening when he rode down from the mountains into Cruces, it seemed to him that miraculous influences had been working on him all the while. He had been seized upon like driftwood by a powerful current, and brought straight down to the moment he desired. Now he was accepted by the family of the man he had killed. All the strength of Monterey and his men would be focused to help him in his work, and he was given freely his opportunity to step into the shoes of the dead man. In a sense, the ghost of young Pedro Monterey was most certainly walking up and down with him.

Other things, small problems, remained to be explained. For one thing, if Bandini had been retained as a tutor to educate Pedro as a fighting man, it was odd that the teacher and the pupil should have been so obviously quarreling when they were in Cruces together. But this was a minor point. The main fact was that at last he was confronting the unfinished life work of the dead man. He could not falter now. But though that work was exactly where his strength was the greatest, he felt assured that there were odds against him too great to be overcome. Monterey, with all of his men, had struggled vainly these many years. It would be strange indeed if he could succeed where so many had failed utterly.

Even when he had been imprisoned he had hardly felt a more intimate sense of peril than that which followed him coldly up and down through this room. And in the

77

background of his brain the thought of the Drummons rose up like thunderheads in a winter sky.

He was still pacing the floor when a tap came at the door, and he opened it on Julia. There seemed to be no light whatever in the hallway. The black hand of darkness held her in sharp relief.

"Is your uncle still holding a stiff upper lip?" asked Silver. "I've never seen a stronger will."

"He's shaking like a leaf now," said the girl. "But he won't let himself think about Pedrillo. He keeps poor Pedro out of his mind. That's the reason why he's able to bear up. And he'll keep fighting back the sorrow, because that alone would be enough to kill him, and he won't die until he's made the Drummons suffer."

Silver nodded. "Señorita," he said, "I want to know a few things."

"I thought you would," she answered. "Ask me."

"About you first. Who are you?"

"I'm the waif, the orphan, the poor relation. My name is Monterey, also."

"You're no more Mexican," said he, "than I am."

"My mother was American," she told him. "That's all about me."

"Your father and your mother died, and Don Arturo took you in?"

"Yes."

"And you've been happy here?"

"Who can be really happy in the Haverhill? There's a curse on the entire valley."

"How close a relation are you of this family?"

"A third cousin."

"And you want to leave the Haverhill and the Casa Monterey?"

"Not until Uncle Arturo is either happy or—dead."

"Tell me about Pedro. Sit down and tell me."

She sat on the edge of a chair. He sat down in turn and took his unshaven, unclean face between his hands.

"Pedro was handsome—but you saw him."

"The finest-looking lad I ever saw."

"And he was the true steel all the way through. He laughed a little too much to please his father. But he had the making of a fine man."

78

"I knew it," said Silver bitterly. "There was no flaw in him, and I—" He finished with a gesture. "Tell me more about him," he urged.

"You only shortened his life a little," she answered. "He was to go against the Drummons in a short time, and they would have crushed him at once. Pedro was not clever. He was not very wise or strong-minded, either. He was simply honest and cheerful and brave. He would not have known how to meet the Drummons. He would have ridden straight at them—and that would have been the end."

Silver lifted his head and looked at her, but he was seeing the face of the dead man again. He felt that it was true—that young Pedro would have charged a mountain blindly.

"There's another thing—Bandini," he said.

"Bandini is a rascal."

"Does Monterey know that?"

"No. Uncle Arturo loves him—simply because he can ride well and shoot straight, and because he pretends to have a deathless devotion to my uncle and his cause. But as a matter of fact, all that he's interested in is in lining his wallet with more money. I'm sure of it. He worked here teaching Pedro how to ride, how to shoot, even how to fight with a knife. It used to be a savage thing to see them fighting, even although the knives were wood! But Uncle Arturo believes in Bandini almost as he believes in the Bible."

"Where will Bandini be now?"

"Taking charge of the body of poor Pedrillo, seeing that it's embalmed, bringing it back toward the Haverhill."

"He'll be here soon?"

"Yes. What else do you want to know?"

His eyes surveyed her face curiously. She was not beautiful, but something from the mind spoke in her face. The lips and chin were modeled with the tender delicacy of childhood still; but across the forehead and eyes she was a woman.

"Only one other thing," said Silvertip. "That's about the servants. They hate me. But will you try to tell them that I'm not a monster?"

"You're wise," she answered. "You're so wise that you'll add a few days to your life, perhaps."

"A few days?" said Silver. "I'll live to be as old as Monterey."

She looked up at him and smiled.

"I hope so," she said, and almost immediately she said good night, and walked off into the thick blackness of the hall with the surety of one born blind and stepping through a familiar place.

Silver closed the door, stripped, took a sponge bath in cold water, and went to bed. The coolness of the sheets soothed him. All the blood of his body seemed to be gathered in his head, and to be whirling and churning there.

He looked to the side out the window. Now that the room was thoroughly darkened, the stars were both brighter and more distant. He watched the patterning in which they were set. By degrees it grew confused. The points of light seemed to be moving a little. They softened, blurred, and Silver was asleep.

CHAPTER XIV

The Sheriff

THE sheriff came up with the sun, so to speak, and old Arturo Monterey and Silver had to go out and meet him on the terrace garden behind the house. Silver had risen to find that fresh clothes were laid out on a chair beside his bed. When he had shaved, he looked at a face four shades paler than it had been for years, and chiseled lean and hard by pain. And then he tried on the clothes and found that they fitted almost miraculously.

But they were Mexican type. There was a tightly fitted jacket, with his big shoulders exploding out above the narrowness of the waist, and there was a sash that went about the hips, and all the middle of his body was incased as in armor, though the trousers flared out at the bottom a little. His own old sombrero looked sadly out of place with such an outfit. There was another hat with the clothes, one with a silver band of Mexican wheelwork girdling the crown, but he could not induce himself to put this on. It was bad enough to be Mexican to the neck; his head had to remain in an American fashion.

He had barely finished dressing when he received the summons to join Monterey in the terrace garden behind the house. He went uneasily, wondering about the cat-footed one who had been able to enter his room unheard during the night and place that outfit at his hand. There the body of Chuck Terry was laid out among the tall flowers exactly where the imprint of it had fallen the night before.

The sheriff considered the situation with a sour eye. He was a true Haverhill man, with the jowls, the blunt jaw and nose, the huge brows that kept the eyes in shadow. And, like the rest of the tribe, it seemed as though the sun could have no power to influence his skin; very few of those men were tanned. The majority, and the sheriff was one of them, kept an unhealthy white, like that of things which seldom see the day. Those Haverhill men all looked as though they were freshly out of prison.

He listened to the story with angry eyes that shifted from the face of Monterey to that of Silver.

"How would you know?" challenged the sheriff. "How would you know that poor Chuck here wasn't just comin' up to make a friendly call?"

"Perhaps that was all he was doing. In that case, we made an unhappy mistake," said Monterey.

The profound irony of this remark influenced even the mind of the sheriff. He kicked the ground and stamped on it impatiently.

"You gents," said the sheriff, "oughta take your time about things. There's been too much shootin' around the Haverhill. And it's gotta stop. *I'm* goin' to stop it. You all hear me? Here comes Chuck. Just kind of curious. He was only a kid. He was younger than his years. Everybody knew that. Just a great big, open-hearted, fine kid. Just curious. Like the way an antelope is curious, the poor fool! And he comes up here with a friend, and they wanta have a look at the great Arturo Monterey. That's all they wanta do. And by thunder, I'm goin' to jail the pair of you for murder, is what I'm goin' to do! There ain't any sense. There ain't right in it. There ain't any judge, and there ain't any jury that wouldn't call it murder!"

"When a fellow's so curious that he and his pal start sneaking up behind a man at night," said Silver, "and when they start shooting as soon as they hear some one behind them sing out—"

"Just kind of startled, maybe," suggested the sheriff. But presently he was scowling at the ground.

Monterey, in that moment, let his eyes run over the new clothes on the body of Silver, and at the new face which had been revealed by the shaving away of the shaggy growth of beard. He seemed to find much that was worth seeing, and his glance wandered intently from feature to feature. To Silver, aware of the survey, it seemed as though the old man were weighing him in a fine balance and accepting him as a thing of price.

"All right," said the sheriff. "I oughta take up the two of you, but there's enough trouble already, and this'll just make more. I'll leave you go free. You, Monterey—and you're the gent called Silver?"

"Yes," said he.

"You're the one with the white horns, are you?" said the sheriff. "Well, young feller, if you'd keep your horns out of this business here in Haverhill Valley, you'd be a lot better off, and so would we. You been makin' trouble, and you're goin' to make a lot more trouble, and before the end, maybe you'll wish that you never seen the Haverhill River, or the Haverhill men that the whole valley had oughta belong to!"

After that he had the body of the dead man placed in his buckboard and drove off, but his venomous eyes dwelt continually on Silver all the time that the preparations were going on; particularly after he had stared for a time at the red spot on the left breast of the coat of Chuck Terry.

"They've laid their eyes on you now, señor," said Monterey, "and that means that the air you breathe in this valley is poisoned from this moment on. But you have a horse, and yonder is the nearest way to the first pass. And in two hours you can be safely over the hills. Think carefully, my friend. Every chance is against us. They have numbers. They have craft. They have the cruelty of devils and the persistence of hungry beasts. Nothing but the last chance is left to you if you remain!"

It was not half-hearted persuasion. As in the eyes of the girl now and again, so in the eyes of Monterey, something came up from the spirit and spoke to Silvertip.

But he slowly shook his head and smiled.

Julia came suddenly out to them from the house. Her

glance found Silver and dwelt on him with a smile. He knew that she had picked the outfit, by the look she gave it.

"I have stopped trying to persuade him," said Monterey. "If he is to stay here, Heaven knows it is of his own free will; and like a gift from Heaven I take him. You have news in your face, Julia. What is it?"

"Juan Perez is a madman," said the girl. "He has bitten his lips till they bleed. I tried to speak to him. But he lay on a bed and kept beating his head with his hands. He says that he is shamed forever. Something will have to be done about him. You must go to him, Uncle Arturo."

"No," said Silver. "I'll go myself."

"You?" she cried. "He will try to kill you! There is a wild devil in him. It's more dangerous to rob a man of his self-respect than to take the cubs from a she-bear."

"I'm the man to see him," said Silver. "Let me go to him."

"Perhaps," said Arturo Monterey. "But I shall go with you. Juan Perez is the most faithful of the faithful, but there never was a more dangerous man."

"Show me to the door of his room," said Silver. "Then leave me there."

The two of them conducted him. They went across the patio and into the long wing where the servants were housed. At the end of the long and narrow upper hall, Arturo Monterey stopped before a door.

"Go back now," said Silver. "Or else stand here quietly. I know how to handle this case. And if I don't manage him now, he'll put a knife in my back later on. Stand quietly, and don't argue. I have to have my way about this."

He knocked at the door. A faint groan answered him. He opened the door and stepped into a naked little room with only the mask of a grizzly hanging on the wall, and the claws of the great bear strung on a half necklace below the head. On a cot lay the tall form of Perez, face down.

"Juan Perez!" said Silver.

The Mexican came to life with a bound. He said nothing. The devil that was in him needed no sound for expression. The writhing face of Juan Perez expressed him fully enough.

The Mexican had thrown off his belt. Now he caught from it the long hunting knife whose handle projected from a leather sheath. The steel flashed in the dim room as Perez leaped.

But Silver put his hands behind his back and waited. The left hand of Perez caught at his throat. The knife trembled with the tense strength of the arm that wielded it. But it was not driven home.

"Will you listen to me?" said Silver.

Juan Perez thrust himself back to arm's length. The gringo was in his power. The point of that knife could find the life with a single slight gesture. But though the Mexican was half mad with shame, there was manliness in him that made it impossible to strike an unresisting enemy.

"Now, gringo—now, dog," he groaned. "Take your gun and fight me man to man!"

"We are serving the same master, Juan Perez," said Silver. "Will he gain very much if we kill one another? The Drummons will laugh; they will be the ones to gain."

"You tore me from my horse in the town; you have beaten me senseless and left me in your own prison; and the people are laughing at me!" cried Juan Perez.

"And you," said Silver, "have thrown me into the slime of a dark cellar, and tossed my bread into the foul water, and left me there to starve and go mad in the dark. Which of us has suffered the most from the other?"

The logic of this statement was so convincing that the left hand of Perez fell away from the collar of Silver's jacket. He retreated a step, breathing very hard. His teeth were set. He seemed striving to work himself again to the height of his passion, but an increasing calmness appeared in his eyes.

"If I forgive you," said Silver, "it will be a greater thing in the eyes of every one than if you forgive me. And that is what I have come to say to you. Let us forgive one another. Let me have your hand. We are each wise enough to know that the other man is worth fear. Therefore he is worth respect. I respect you, Juan Perez. I want you for my friend. That is why I have come here. That is why I humble myself and take the first long steps. They told me that you would kill me the instant that I appeared, but I knew that you are an honorable man. Here is my hand, Perez. Give me yours!"

"And how about my shame?" muttered Perez. "The smiles? The sneers?"

"I have seen a great many brave men in the world," said Silver, "but I don't know one brave enough to sneer or smile when he sees Juan Perez and Silver walking shoulder to shoulder as friends."

Juan Perez suddenly clasped the hand of Silver. The other hand of the Mexican was struck against his forehead.

"What am I doing?" he exclaimed. "Have my wits gone?"

"Is it a foolish thing," said Silver, "to turn an enemy into a friend? Are you afraid of what old women will say, or do you want the friendship of true men?"

"You are right," said Perez, taking his breath in great gulps. "There is no more truth in all the blue sky than in what you have said. But let me be alone for a little longer. Let me prepare myself. Then I shall walk out into the open day and take your hand where every one can see us. And if there are smiles—"

He ground his teeth together at the thought. Silver dropped a hand on his shoulder.

"This is the beginning, brother," said he. "Before the end of the trail, we shall have ridden through some strange places together. Come when you wish. Call for me if you please. I am in your service and you are in mine, and we shall fight for the same master. Adios!"

He went out of the room, and down the hall he saw the Montereys standing side by side. To their astonished eyes, he smiled and waved; and when he joined them, old Monterey exclaimed:

"What has happened?"

"We have shaken hands," said Silver. "We are now brothers. We shall go to one another whenever we are called, and we shall serve one master."

He went down the stairs before them. And he heard Monterey saying:

"You understand, Julia? As I said before, it is not chance. There is fate in it. If Juan Perez is won over, then all the others will be ready to follow him. They will

86

ride behind him just as though he were my own son and wore my proper name!"

Silver went back to his own room, and there a servant brought him fresh chocolate, and bread, baked in small brown loaves, with butter. He ate and drank hungrily. There was a full pot of frothed chocolate, and he drained it to the last sip. Then he smoked a cigarette and watched the wreaths of blue-white rising up against the ceiling. He could think of nothing except the round, brown face of Tonio for the purpose he had in mind. Tonio to-day—Juan Perez on other occasions.

So he went out into the patio and sent for Tonio. The minute the man appeared, Silver knew that his interview with Perez had become known, for there was no hostility in the big eyes.

The eyes of Tonio were pale and a little prominent. They blinked twice as he greeted Silver. Then he began to smile.

"Tonio, will you help me to-day?" asked Silver.

"There is nothing every one on the place wishes except to serve the señor," said Tonio. "For my part, no trouble would be too great; we know what service was done the night before in the garden terrace."

"You'll help me then, Tonio?" asked Silver. "The first thing is to take me out riding and show me the way to the house of Henry Drummon. Will you do that?"

Tonio's round fat face wrinkled like the skin of an overripe apple.

Then he sighed and nodded. But he added: "This is war now, señor."

He waved his hand at the breadth of the valley, the pale-green of the grass, with the wind and the sun giving it a shimmering life, and the trees rolling in darker clouds across it.

"War now," said Tonio. "There has been almost peace for these last years, but now there is another death, and the war commences once more. If we go to look at the Drummons, be sure that the Drummons are coming to look at us. There will be cattle rustling, horse stealing, and every rock, and every stump, and every bush will have a rifle behind it, perhaps. But if you wish to ride to see the Drummons, I'll show you the way."

They went to the stable, where Silver found his mustang. In the patio, the girl came out to watch them leave. She had on a wide-brimmed straw hat, tipped so that the brim was a halo for her face; and she wore a blue dress with yellow Mexican embroidery spilling across it.

Silvertip waited for her to say something, but she said nothing at all. She merely came out to the patio entrance and watched them go through the arch. The sun flamed on the whitewash of the wall behind her as she watched them pass. Silver turned suddenly to speak to her; the words stuck in his throat; he rode on silently. There was something fixed and still about her smile, and a pallor around the mouth that told him she was smiling merely as a soldier smiles when he faces the firing squad. Perhaps she was guessing what errand he rode on with Tonio. Perhaps she was assuring herself that neither of them would ever come back again.

Juan Perez was gone with Monterey; Tonio was with Silver; no one remained in the house to give guidance to the ignorant, clumsy peons, and the unruly vaqueros who could protect her in case the Drummons, in fact, were reaching out at that moment toward the house of Monterey.

But he went on.

"Gallop, Tonio!" he called, and they raced down the slope and swung down the easy pitch toward the middle of the valley, then out from it into the broader expanse of the Haverhill Valley itself.

Presently, when their horses were black with sweat, they drew rein at a signal from Tonio. His lifted hand pointed toward a group of cattle that seemed to Silver a smaller and a scrawnier breed, less square in the quarters than the stock of Monterey.

"You see the brand? You know it?" asked Tonio.

Silver singled out a steer and drifted slowly down toward it, until he made out the loom and strike of the brand against the skin of one of the quarters.

"Bar 17 Bar?" called he to Tonio. "Is that the brand?"

"That's it. That's the Drummon brand."

Silver looked around him with an appreciative eye. He could understand that in the Drummon range it was necessary to go on more carefully.

"Where did the men of this valley come from?" he asked.

Tonio made a great gesture toward the east.

"A long time ago they were in England, some people that looked like beasts, I suppose," said Tonio. "Then they move out and go to Carolina. They go back up into mountains. They stay there till their neighbors begin to hunt them like beef. They leave that country and they go West. They come to the valley here. They kill the Haverhills, who own half the valley. They start fighting the Montereys. They keep on fighting the Montereys. Now there is one old man left to us, and there are plenty of Drummons remaining. They stay all the same. When strangers come into the valley, the Drummons ride them down. They burn the houses the squatters build. Sometimes they burn the squatters with the houses."

"And nothing is done to 'em?" asked Silver.

"The sheriff is Drummon, the jury is Drummon, the judge is Drummon," said Tonio calmly.

Then his eyes rolled, and his teeth flashed in something that was not a smile.

"Before I die, I shall do something!" said Tonio. "I have already done a little bit in my life!"

He held up one finger as he spoke, and drew in his breath through his teeth, as though he were drinking.

He had killed at least one Drummon; that was fairly clear.

"How many have gone down in the fighting?" asked Silvertip. He took off his hat and ran his hand over his head as he waited for the answer.

"Who knows?" asked Tonio cheerfully. "Fifty years— and who knows? When I was a boy there were two other little towns in the valley. They were both Mexican towns. Now they are gone. The fire caught hold of them on windy nights, and they're both gone. Look there—by the edge of the river—yonder!"

Silver could see it—a curious dark smudge, covered with small mounds.

"That was one of them. That was the last one. The grass hasn't begun to grow on them yet," said Tonio. "There is only Haverhill now. But who can tell? Some night the wind may blow *up* the valley, and there may be fire in *that* wind; and then there will be no Haverhill town, either."

He began to laugh and nod. And Silvertip saw the picture of the flames whirling, and the houses dissolving, and the people running into the night, dragging with them what they were trying to save from the ruin, and clouds of sparks exploding up into the sky.

Perhaps he would have to see that picture painted brightly in before he came to the end of his days.

CHAPTER XV

The Drummon Place

THEY came to the verge of the bright water, with its currents running like half-luminous shadows beneath the surface.

"This is the limit," said Tonio. "This is as far as we can go. Over there is the home of Henry Drummon—beyond that hill, with the trees covering it. If any of the men of Monterey are found across this river, we are shot like dogs. It is the dead line."

"We could ford the stream right here, I think," said Silver.

"Yes," said Tonio, "and we could be shot on the other bank."

Silver scanned the wooded head of that hill and knew perfectly that he would have to cross to the other side of it. He knew, rising in him, the peculiar force of the temptation, and he set his teeth against the surge of it in vain.

At last he said: "We'd better go over to have a bit of a look, Tonio, don't you think so?"

Tonio stared at him.

"This," he said, making an appropriate gesture, "is the

dead line." He indicated the river with the sweep of his hand, and continued by drawing the edge of the hand across his throat suddenly. "Besides," he said, "this is the daylight. And they are all hawks and owls. They can see miles and miles even in the half light. What do you wish to do, señor?"

Silver drew up his belt a notch, as though he were hungry.

"I'll go over and take a look at the house," he said. "Go back in there among those trees, Tonio, and wait for me. If you hear guns, and don't see me come pelting back over the head of that hill, you'll know that they've got me, and you won't have to wait any longer."

Tonio shouted in rapid protest, but Silver was already riding into the water. He would not look back, in spite of the heated arguments that Tonio poured into his ears from a distance. But when he gained the farther bank, he turned and waved his hand. Tonio, with both arms moving, was indicating to heaven and earth that he abandoned the cause of a madman. Silver cantered his mustang up the easy slope and made straight at the hill.

As he came to it, he swung the horse to the side, and well away from a road that cleft through the trees. He had barely changed direction when he heard the beating of many hoofs, the creaking of leather, the notes of raised voices. And as the trees began to spread their branches above him, he saw a cavalcade of half a dozen riders sweep over the top of the hill, with a cluster of dogs racing about the horses, or frolicking in the lead.

It was a group of the Drummons. He could have known them at a greater distance by the way the big, blocky heads were set on the thick necks, and by the way the necks grew out of the shoulders. He could have judged, too, by something devil-may-care in the free swing of their riding. The very dogs had a look that to Silver seemed harmonious in the entire picture. They were huge brutes, all of a type, and the type something between wolfhound and mastiff.

When he came to a good thickness of brush, Silver dropped from the saddle, threw the reins, and made sure that he was well hidden from the eye of any observer. With a rattle and a roar, the group went by down the road.

He breathed more easily, and was about to toss the reins over the head of the sweating mustang again when a hound gave tongue on a note that approached him rapidly.

A voice yelled out of the distance: "Belle! Hey, Belle, you brindle-faced fool, stop running that rabbit track! Come back here, Belle!"

But the baying of the dog still approached, and now a great brute with a brindled head and a white-and-tan body broke through the shrubbery, hesitated, then hurled itself straight at Silver.

He aimed at the head of Belle a kick that missed but made her swerve. Her bared teeth almost gripped his leg. As he turned, she was swerving, leaping full at his head. Instinct made him reach both hands forward, and luck gave him a double handhold just under the jaws. He let the big dog swing with the impetus of its own leap and flung her heavily on her back, his own weight behind the fall.

She lay still, on her side, with her long red tongue lolling out onto the dust and no sign of motion in her sides. He was afraid for an instant that she was dead, and if her master found her stretched out, he would not pause until he had found the cause that had brained her.

Through the trees, through the shrubbery, a horse was crashing its way, and the voice of the master was roaring:

"Belle, you woodenheaded fool! Belle! Come here! Hey, Belle! I'm going to have the hide off you; I'm going to have it off with a whip!"

The dog revived all in an instant. Once on her feet, she stood swaying for a moment, her red eyes fixed eagerly on Silvertip; then she swung to the side and went hurtling away toward the calling voice.

Silver heard the man cursing. They were so close that he could even make out the whistling of the whip with which he struck at the dog. Then all those noises receded. He heard the pounding of hoofs, and the high-pitched halloo of the rider, hastening after his mates.

Silvertip took the loop of the reins over his arm and walked on among the trees slowly, scanning the vistas which opened among the trunks, and swerved away and closed to either side. He went on until he reached the brow of the hill. The trees stopped there suddenly. Through the verge of them he glimpsed a picture still obscured and brown-striped by the tree trunks which intervened between him and the open.

He saw a shallow valley, with a crooked flash of water streaked across the center of it, trees clustering here and there, and a long, low-fronted house that had once been painted white, though now the weather had scraped the wood bare in most places, and left merely a look of wet dust. The tramping of many hoofs had worn away all grass near the house, and across the face of the building stretched a hitch rack whose beams had been gnawed thin in many places. The front door was set off by an ornamental hood of carved wood, and there was a brass knocker that looked foolishly out of place.

Silvertip left his mustang and rounded to the rear of the house. A narrow veranda ran along it. A workbench had been rigged here by laying a few long boards across two sawbucks. On the bench appeared the keel and the ribs of a sharp-ended rowboat which was probably intended for the stream that ran down the hollow near the house, and not for the Haverhill Valley itself. There was a litter of wood shavings on the floor, and spilling off onto the ground. From pegs along the outer wall hung bits of harness, and coats and hats mostly green with age, as though they had been hung up one day and then forgotten during years.

Silvertip tapped at the open kitchen door. He could see no one inside—only the worn tatters of some linoleum on the floor, and a broom with half the straw scrubbed from it, and a big rusty range on which a few pots were steaming idly. But a stifled voice called from an unseen corner of the room, and Silver went in.

In a corner near the sink, at a little kitchen table, sat a lad of fifteen, chewing at a big mutton bone, ripping off the shreds of flesh, or gnawing at the knuckle with strong, white teeth. He kept on gnawing, his eyes half closed with content, half buried by the upward snarling of his face muscles. Even at fifteen, he had the perfect Drummon features beneath a ragged mop of hair. He continued to chew at the bone, mumbling around it:

"Who're you?"

"I'm a new man," said Silver, and walked over to the

stove, where he lifted the lid, replenished the fire box with wood, and thrust the heavy poker into the rising of the flames. With the lids replaced, except one which the poker shaft lifted askew, Silver turned toward young Drummon and found that the latter, having put down his bone for a moment, was licking his chops and staring with insolent eyes. He looked as dangerous as a half-grown mountain lion; and one could be sure that he was far more formidable than that.

"You're the new man, are you?" asked young Drummon.

"Yes. I'm the new man."

"The devil you are. There *ain't* any new man."

"You ask your old man," said Silver.

"Whatcha mean? That a way of telling me to go to the devil?"

"Why? Is he dead?" said Silver.

"Yeah. Sure, he's dead. The greasers got him. But I'm goin' to get me a coupla yaller skunks to make up before I'm a lot older. What's your name? Who are you?"

"I'm a fellow that keeps my mouth shut," said Silver, "and never asks a lot of questions, and doesn't answer 'em, either."

"You don't, don't you?" asked the lad, rising.

He showed six feet and an inch of tough muscle laid over a burly frame. His neck was already as thick as a wrestler's; and his pale Drummon eyes glared at Silvertip.

"You're goin' to talk, or you're goin' to get out," said young Drummon. "If Alligator Hank was here, he'd know if you was one of the real men. But he ain't far away, and I could call him. But I don't need to call him. Whatcha doin' with that poker? Back up and lemme hear you chatter! I mean it. Turn around here and talk or I'm goin' to sock you."

The voice of the lad was rising as he spoke. It reached a high-pitched snarl at this moment, and he leaped with no further warning at Silver. Silver was loath to strike. But it was not defending himself against a boy so much as against a dangerous young beast of prey. He let the hard-driven fist of Drummon go past his head, and clipped him on the chin as he swayed forward.

The hair flew up on the head of the youth. He stood

rocking, with blank eyes. Silver took him under the armpits, led him to the door, and thrust him outside. He walked away with drunken, fumbling steps, and Silver, turning back to the stove, drew out the poker.

It was white-hot, throwing out a shower of coruscations. He went through the house and opened the front door. On the solid face of it he fulfilled the first vow of old Arturo Monterey by searing into the wood the sign of the Cross, with the wavering line of the Snake underneath it.

CHAPTER XVI

The Pursuit

HE RETRACED the line of the Snake with the tip of the poker, now a dull red, and heard from the rear of the house a loud shouting, answered from not far off. Silver threw the poker away and ran for the woods where his mustang was left. He had hoped that all the Drummon men would be in the party which he had watched ride out hunting. But, as in a hornet's nest, there appeared to be a continual reserve of warriors about the camp. For now he heard the thudding of hoofs, and he looked back as the big youngster, running on foot, turned the corner of the house with three horsemen sweeping up behind him.

They were Drummons, every one, and the central figure of the three bore a face which Silvertip would never forget. It was the true Drummon type, with fleshy, battered brow, and skull-like eyes, but the neck and the features of the man were flushed over and swollen with whisky bloat, like a raw sunburn.

He led the way, and, pointing to the side, toward the front door of the house, uttered a sudden wild yell of rage. For he had seen the newly drawn brand!

Silver was already inside the brush. It crashed and crackled around him. A rapid fire of bullets searched it, also. One of them nicked the mustang as Silver mounted. It reared, struck out at the air, then fled unmanageably among the trees. There was more danger from its running than from the gunfire to the rear. The branches of the trees seemed to reach out and then stoop suddenly at the head of the rider. The tree trunks threatened to strike him on either side and fling him with a broken body to the ground.

At last, sawing savagely at the reins, he managed to get the head of the frightened horse under control. They were already nearing the edge of the woods; now they swept out into the open, and Silvertip saw a cavalcade coming up on the farther side of the river, the same rout of horsemen and dogs that had streamed past him not long before. But there was one difference now. For in the midst of them, his hands tied behind his back, rode Tonio.

The distance was still great, but by the horse Silver knew his companion. The little mustang went proudly along, as though feeling that it was a guard of honor that accompanied its master. But the sight was a stroke to the very heart of Silvertip. For Tonio had protested; he had not come blindly into the region of danger, but had been persuaded and drawn on against his will.

Retreat in the direction of the river was impossible. Silver turned the horse back into the trees. The three riders, yelling loudly, poured into the open, had a glimpse of him, and hurtled in pursuit again.

He ran the horse hard, so that the brush cracked noisily about him. Then, making a sudden halt, he turned to the side and walked the mustang a few quiet steps into high brush.

It might be that he could lose them in that way. He heard them come with a sweep; he saw, through the screen of branches, shadowy forms leaping past him, two of them in succession. But a third drove straight at his place of concealment. Only chance was aiming that course; but it came near to being the death of Silvertip. He had to get his mustang under way with a rush, swerving it well to the side.

It was the man of the bloated face, looking redder than

ever because of the white flash of his bared teeth as he fired on Silver. The first bullet sang at the ear of Silver; the second knocked the hat from his head.

"Alligator—hey, Hank—you got him?" yelled a voice from in front.

"I've nicked him. Turn to the right and we'll bag him. We got him! He's the one that killed Terry!"

But Silvertip's mustang already had taken him clear of the woods. He took an angling course to the right, down the slope of the hill. The guns began again behind him. Then the trees of an open grove received him, flicking back in a shadowy throng, like the pickets of a fence.

That patch of trees shielded him from gunfire for a little distance. He reached the small stream in the center of the hollow at a narrows, and the mustang leaped the gap. On the farther slope he gained another cluster of trees.

The Drummons were not gaining. They had been too eager with their guns, and a man cannot shoot and ride his best at the same time. They gave up gun work now. Their hat brims blown and flapping like open jaws, they came now with a rush; and off to the side, from the big barn behind the house, the youngster was quirting a mustang into full speed, trying to cut across the line of the flight.

Silvertip angled again to the right. There were more trees in clusters that received him as clouds in the sky receive a fugitive bird when the hawks are flying near.

Then the mouth of a narrow canyon opened to his left. He shot into it. A yell of frenzied delight rang behind him, to give warning that he was in a trap, and, scudding around the next corner, he saw the very face of the danger. For the ravine ended against a sheer wall of rock fifty feet high, with a dribble of water dropping into mist from the lip of the rock.

He snatched the rifle from its saddle holster and leaped to the ground while the mustang was still running.

To the left the wall of the ravine went up like the flat of a hand; to the right a rubble and scattering of great boulders climbed in broken stairs toward the sky line. Silver was instantly in the heart of that rocky confusion.

The Drummons were already at the spot. They were

out of the saddle; they were pouring in among the big boulders, calling directions.

Silver lay out on the flat forehead of a rock and waited. A head bobbed at the side of a great stone twenty yards beneath him.

He knocked the hat off that head. Another man lurched into view and dodged back to shelter again with a yelp; a bullet from Silver's gun had slipped through his arm.

Then Silver continued his retreat, for he knew that they would not press him too closely. Twice he came into the open; twice they salted the rocks around him with splashes of lead. But he was not touched in body. He had lost a hat; his coat was torn with a great gash close to the pit of his right arm; and that was the only mark he bore.

He reached the top of the divide. Beneath him was another valley; or he could go up or down the divide itself. But he chose, as an alternative, to double back down the hillside which he had just climbed. He could hear the gritting of heels among the stone. So he pulled off his riding boots and feathered his way among the boulders in his stockinged feet.

Just before him he heard the grunt and stifled gasp of a man doing hard labor. Silver dropped to a knee with his gun ready. The sun beat on him with sudden strength. He was aware of the gleaming of the rocks around him. For an instant all of that great face of nature was still, and all its eyes seemed to be focused upon him.

He waited with his teeth set behind that faint smile of his. If the fellow who puffed and panted among the rocks so close to him came in view, there would have to be a death. His own position among the rocks would be revealed, and the others could take him from above and hunt him down with ease.

But the hurrying climber went by on the left, out of view. And Silvertip continued to work down among the rocks.

Above him he heard voices ring out; then the sounds grew dim, as though the Drummons had clambered into the valley just beyond them.

He reached the floor of the ravine. Looking up, he saw one form looking gigantic against the sky, rifle at the ready, as the lookout turned gradually, scanning all about him.

Yet he never looked down into the floor of the canyon, where Silvertip was now stealing toward his mustang.

He gained the saddle before a yell from the middle of the sky, as it seemed, floated down to him; then bullets. Those bullets merely helped him. Nothing is harder than to shoot accurately from a height at a running target. The gunfire aided Silver to rouse the four other horses to a frenzy of panic, and they scattered at full speed before him down the canyon, out into the pleasant, open green of the valley.

There was no more pursuit. There *could* be no more. He caught up those four Drummon horses, fastened their lead ropes together, and trotted straight back toward the house of Monterey.

Nothing happened on the way. He saw not a soul. Nothing lived in the valleys except the slowly browsing cattle, or the bright wind riffles that ran over the grass.

So he came up the narrower valley into view of the fortress house of Monterey. It seemed to him like a picture of a gallant last stand, a great castle without a garrison. There were armed men within, to be sure, but at their head was a tired, grim, despairing old man.

He came up to the patio gate; and there a house *mozo* greeted him, stared at the horses, then saw the brands on their sides, and gave token of news to the entire household with a yell.

CHAPTER XVII

In the Night

IT WAS like the alarming of a garrison, indeed. Distant shouts, distant footfalls beat inside the house; doors slammed like muffled reports of cannon; then the torrent of humanity came sweeping out into the patio. Male and female, they gathered about the four captured horses; they examined the bleeding cut where a bullet had nicked Silver's mustang across the quarters. They laid their fingers on the shot-torn cantle of his saddle. They noted the absence of his hat, and they looked with a deep interest on the torn side of his coat. But even more than these signs of battle, they regarded the horses of the Drummons with a sort of startled awe, at first, but afterward with a joyous laughter.

Julia Monterey came out, last of all, and Silvertip told her, shortly:

"Tonio's gone. We got to the river, and I wanted to go across to see the Drummon house. Tonio hid and waited for me. I went on to the house, and burned the brand on the door of it. The Drummons chased me. The head of the gang was with the rest. They hunted me up to the rocks.

I managed to get around 'em and bring back the horses. And I saw a whole herd of the Drummons leading Tonio up to the Drummon house. It's a bad business, Julia. And there's the whole of it."

Tonio? It seemed as though his life or death were of no interest at all to the other Mexicans, compared with the immense fact that the first step of Monterey's vow had been performed. That vow was known to the whole world, it appeared. It was the battle song which the Monterey faction followed. They were like happy children. Three of the vaqueros rode in from the upper valley, heard the news, and turned the demonstration into a frenzy.

Silvertip escaped into the house. He went out onto the garden terrace at the back of the house with Julia, and a house *mozo* brought out a decanter of strong wine and another of rye whisky. Silver took the whisky. He drank it in small sips, letting the sick burn of it fume in his nose and up like a mounting smoke into his brain. It was bright and hot on the open terrace, but he would not move into the skeleton shade which the pergola offered to them. Instead, he chose to soak in the sunshine, relaxed, inert.

The girl sat opposite him with the same broad hat on her head. At a distance, it buried her features in shadow. At close hand, the color burned through from her cheeks, and her eyes. Her eyes were not Mexican black. They were paler, clearer. There seemed to be more of spirit and less of race in them.

Arturo Monterey walked back and forth across the terrace. He had not spoken a word to Silver about the branding of the door of the Drummons. What he felt about the accomplishment of the first portion of his vow was too great for speech. But as he walked back and forth, once he paused and dropped his hand on the shoulder of the American. Then he continued pacing, and halting at the farther end of the terrace, he stood staring over the lowlands beyond, lost in a dream of hope.

"He even forgets Pedro," said the girl softly. "Don't doubt that he loved his son, but a thousand children would be nothing to him compared with the filling of his vow. Twenty-five years of hating and hoping!"

"And Tonio?" said Silvertip.

103

The sun that blazed on his head made the gray tufts above his temples glisten like metal indeed.

"Tonio? What does he matter?" asked the girl. She laughed bitterly. "Tonio was simply an old adherent, the wisest and the best man in the whole valley, the kindest to me, the truest to his master, the most faithful to his friends. But it doesn't matter. What does the life of one man mean, compared with putting the mark on the door of the Drummon house? Oh, nothing at all!"

She fell silent. He watched the pinching of her lips and the slight flaring of her nostrils. The battle spirit was in her, also, he could see. And out of the distance, he could hear the Mexicans singing. The noise sometimes drove close to them with the opening of a door, then receded, and grew as far away as a thought.

Her chin was dropped on one brown fist that was whitened at the knuckles by the force with which she gripped it. His head was far back; she watched the faintness of his smile.

She looked at him with a queer mixture of horror and admiration.

"You want trouble," she said. "You live by it."

"I'll die by it, too," said Silvertip gloomily.

"What gave you the gray markings in your hair?" she asked. "That wasn't just chance, was it?"

"No. It's a long story," he told her. "Stop talking about me. I want to know about Tonio. What'll they do to him?"

"He'll disappear, that's all. He'll never be seen by his friends again."

"They'll kill him out of hand, eh?"

"Not at all," she answered. "He'll simply be riding through the woods, and he'll brain his head against a bough of a tree. Or else he'll fall off his horse and drown in the rapids. Or he might even have an accident with his own revolver. There are lots of ways. The Drummons won't know anything about it."

He nodded. "Tonio," said Silvertip, "you think quite a lot of him, don't you?"

"He taught me to ride," she said. "He taught me to shoot. He taught me the old Mexican and Indian legends of everything. Whatever I know that's worth knowing, he taught me."

Silvertip nodded again.

"That means I have to get him back," he said.

At this, she looked him over quizzically, dropping her glance from his eyes to his smile. Then she seemed to rally to a sudden realization that he meant what he had said.

"How could you do it? How could you even try to do it?" she asked.

He looked at the horizon line, where it slid up and down the ragged sides of the mountains, across the valley.

"You can't go with numbers; they'd be seen," said she. "And if you go alone, how do you dream you could take Tonio away from them? They know that he's important to Arturo Monterey. They'll keep him caged and watched all the time."

"I'll go off and think," said Silvertip.

He went to his room to be alone. But the four walls looked in upon his mind like four faces.

He went up to the roof of the old house, where a low wall was built around an open promenade. There he remained for hours, smoking cigarettes, staring at the mountains, growing constantly more nervous and tense.

Something was gathering in him, as water gathers behind a dam; something was kindling in him. His smile was seen no more. As the evening came nearer, he began to pace the roof restlessly with a step longer and more silent. He watched the evening begin, the color burn up in the west like a red thunderhead.

Then he went down to the dining room and sat silently at one end of the long table, Monterey at the other, the girl between. She tried to talk; Silver answered in murmurs. The windows grew black with night, the yellow image of the table lamp sitting deep in the glass.

At last he left her, suddenly, and felt the drift of her eyes, as her glance followed him across the room. He knew that she understood where he was going, but she said nothing. An American girl would have had to speak, but the Mexican blood was enough to keep her silent. He felt, at that moment, that to look into her mind would be to look into a greater darkness than the night.

Outside, he went to the stable. Two vaqueros appeared from nowhere and attached themselves to him. Their attitude was a queer mixture of suspicion and respect. He wanted a horse, a fresh horse. They took him with a lantern into the corral behind the stable, and flashed the light for him over the string of mustangs that were kept on hand.

He picked a bay gelding, built long and low, with a pair of fine shoulders. He had not made a mistake; he knew that by the way the two looked at one another. They roped that mustang, together with another, at his request. They wielded long, rawhide lariats, heavy and supple as quicksilver, and made their casts with a queer underhand flick, effortless and sure. The rawhide noose stuck with a report, like the slap of a hand.

The pair were saddled. Silvertip's rifle was brought, examined by one of the vaqueros, and slid into the saddle holster. The Mexicans escorted him to the gate of the patio. They held up their lantern to light him on his way; he saw the flash of their teeth and their eyes, and the gleam of perspiration on their dark faces. Then he was gone down the road.

A voice called after him. As he halted, Juan Perez galloped up and drew rein with a jerk.

"You are riding alone, amigo," said Juan Perez. "How is that? It is too dark to see anything. It is too dark to find anything except trouble. Let me go with you!"

"No," said Silver. "This is a case, Juan, where two men are too many, and where one is almost too much. But when the right time comes, I shall call on no one but you, amigo."

He left Juan Perez sitting the saddle disconsolately, and went on along the road.

He passed a small group of bushes. A figure rose out of it.

"Who goes?" called a voice. And it added instantly: "Señor Silver?"

"Yes!" said Silvertip.

"Good fortune!" called the voice.

Silver rode on. At the mouth of the ravine, two more shadows arose, hailed him, let him pass. It was clear that the men of Monterey would keep good watch.

He kept steadily on across the valley of the Haverhill. The stirrups had been tied up so that they would not flop and make a noise. But as he drew near the ford of the river, the hoofbeats of his mustang seemed to grow louder and louder, for they were entering the domain of the Drummons, and armed men might grow up out of the ground at any moment.

He rode into the ford. The water dashed about the two horses; it seemed to burn with a white fire, to the excited eye of Silvertip. His long-geared mustang grunted as it climbed the farther bank, and it seemed to Silvertip that the sound must reverberate to the very edge of the hills.

But still there was no sign of an enemy.

So he reached the trees that covered the hill before the house of Drummon. There he dismounted, and led the horses slowly through the double blackness beneath the branches until, from the brow of the slope, he saw the long line of lights across the face of the Drummon house. It was not so much like a private dwelling as a hotel.

Many men had gathered; it was no wonder that every room seemed to be lighted. More than a dozen horses were tethered at the hitch rack, hanging their heads patiently, each of them pointing one rear hoof.

He saw the details as he went forward, after throwing the reins of his own pair. He had to move slowly enough to allow the casual eye small chance of seeing him, but there were eyes far from casual now sweeping the night. He saw one dull silhouette of a man move against the wall of the house. Another approached from the left and joined the first at the corner. Silver lay flat in the dust and waited. A tall clump of grass sheltered him.

He heard the voices challenge one another quietly: "All well?" and the answer: "All well."

"It ain't so well for the greaser," said one, and chuckled. "And is he goin' to hold out?"

"Not when Hank Drummon gets working on him."

The two separated, and drifted away, passing dimly down the wall of the house again. Silver, setting his teeth, contemplated a retreat, for it seemed obvious that he would not be able to come closer to a place so well-guarded.

He turned his head and looked back; it seemed to him that the ground over which he had wormed his way was clearly lighted by the stars, and that retreat was almost as dangerous as to advance. Twice more, he saw the sentries meet at the corner, and separate again; and now he got to feet and hands, and went rapidly forward.

The fellow who moved to the right, toward the back of the house, was his goal. The ghostlike footfall of Silver followed him to the end of his beat; and as the man turned, swinging carelessly about, Silvertip laid the muzzle of a revolver against his breast.

"What kind of a fool game is this, Jerry?" asked the guard. "What kind of tricks are you up to, you fool?"

"Hoist your hands, and keep walking," said Silvertip, "and don't speak out loud again. I'm from the house of Monterey."

He heard a sound out of the choking throat of the other. The hands went up slowly. When they were shoulder-high, they paused; and the fellow groaned, faintly, as he struggled between fear and a desire to fight back.

But at last he surrendered, and walked on toward the corner of the house. The rapid hand of Silvertip already had taken the gun that hung in the thigh holster.

"To that other hombre you meet at the corner, I'm Jerry," said Silvertip. "You don't stop to talk to him. You turn around, and walk back with me. We've something to talk about."

Beyond the dark line of the corner of the house stepped the second guard.

"Thought I heard you sing out, Bud?" said he.

"Yeah. Here's Jerry got something to talk over with me," said "Bud," and turned on his heel, with Silver swinging around beside him.

"Jerry?" exclaimed the first guard. "Looks like Jerry had growed a few inches since supper-time. Hey, wait a minute!"

But they walked on slowly. The left hand of Silver kept a firm grip on the arm of his companion. He felt the big muscles slip up and down, like snakes moving beneath the skin. He felt the tremor of shame and disgust that worked in his companion.

"Stop here!" commanded Silver.

They were just under a lighted window, shuttered fast, the lamplight working dimly through the cracks. But one leaf of the shutter was broken out, and since it was fairly close to the level of the eye of Silvertip, he could look into the room. It was fairly crowded with a dozen or more men. He saw first the red of the whisky-bloated face of that Drummon who had helped to hunt him on this same day. And now he saw Tonio, tied to a chair and directly confronting the window outside of which Silvertip stood.

The man of the red, swollen face stood beside the prisoner, with his arms folded.

"Who is it?" asked Silvertip. "The older one—with the red mug?"

"Him?" muttered Bud. "That's Hank. That's Hank himself."

Silver looked into the puffed brutality of those features with a lingering and curious horror.

He heard a thick voice, husky and powerful, that matched the look of the man, saying: "All right, Tonio. This is the night when we ride at the house of Monterey. You go along and show us where the guards may be, and save your hide. We been handlin' you with gloves, Tonio, but now I'm goin' to cut deeper'n the skin. Are you swingin' over to our side?"

Tonio leaned his head back a trifle and laughed in the face of Drummon.

CHAPTER XVIII

The Torture Job

IT SEEMED to Silvertip incredible that any human being could show such immense assurance, such carelessness of his life, as to insult Henry Drummon at such a time. The whole roomful of men surged toward the prisoner, but the older man and leader held up his hand and checked the advance.

"You ain't goin' to help us, eh, Tonio?" he said.

Tonio was silent.

"It wouldn't be much to do," declared Drummon. "All we want is to have the posts of the guards pointed out to us. And the entrance to the cellar under the house. That ain't much to do. We don't ask you to help in the fight, because we want all of that for ourselves. You hear me, Tonio?"

Tonio yawned. A bystander lifted a gun butt to strike into the captive's face, but again the chief of the clan checked his followers.

"This ain't a time or a place for us to make any hurry," he said. "We gotta think this over. We gotta get the best ideas to use on Tonio. He's goin' to be worth 'em, and he's goin' to last for a while. Get the Runt in. He's the one that will have the best ideas."

Some one laughed loudly—a long, braying sound of pleasure—and strode out of the room slamming the door behind him with such force that it sent a deep vibration down the slender iron chain which supported a lamp above the center table. The table was large and massive, and looked as though it could seat twenty men; and the varnished surface shone under the glare from the great double burner above.

Silvertip, marking that slender chain that held the lamp, felt, for the first time, that perhaps he would not be forced to stand as an idle spectator of the horror which he knew was about to come. For he had no doubt that Henry Drummon intended to torture Tonio to death by the most lingering means possible. And now, as he studied the place where the iron chain met the ceiling, between the two white circles of light above the lamp, there was the glimmering of a hope in him, a vague and far-off thing.

A footfall came toward them from the left; it was the second guard come to inquire into the reason that kept his companion still.

"Send him back," said Silver to Bud. "Curse him out, and send him back."

The other had come almost up to them, when Bud turned fiercely on him.

"Get back on your own beat," commanded Bud. "What the devil you doin' on my side of the house?"

"What's the matter with you?" asked the second guard. He recoiled a little as he spoke. "You act crazy, Bud! What the devil has Jerry put into your head? Has he been talkin' about me?"

"Never mind," growled Bud. "Get out of here, and leave my side of the house, or I'll climb your frame."

"You will, will you?" said the other angrily. He paused for a moment, swaying a little forward, as though he were about to hurl himself at Bud. But caution came gradually over him.

"I'll be seein' you to-morrow about this," he declared. "If somebody finds out that you ain't been walkin' your beat, you'll have your explainin' to do, first, and your fight with me, afterward."

He retreated, however. And Bud, leaning against the wall of the house, groaned softly, in his anguish; but the muzzle of Silvertip's gun was constantly pressed against his ribs.

Inside the room, the Drummons were waiting for the coming of the "Runt." The pause was filled with odd conversation.

"How much Spanish in you, Tonio?" asked Hank Drummon.

"Yo soy puro Indio," said the Mexican, lifting his head a bit.

"I thought so," said Drummon. "It takes an Indian to stand what you're goin' to have to stand. But listen to me —Monterey ain't Indian. There ain't no blood in him except Spanish. Why d'you stick to him in a pinch like this? Can you tell me that?"

Tonio's round face grew flushed, and his eyes glimmered.

"Because the Señor Monterey is father and uncle and brother to me," he answered. "And if all the gringos, and all their lands, and all their money were offered to me instead, I would rather be a slave to the Cross and Snake brand."

Two or three of the Drummons cursed Tonio savagely, but Hank Drummon merely laughed. He seemed to gain a great contentment out of this scene, and now he walked up and down and back and forth, chuckling and rubbing his great red hands together.

With fascinated eyes, Silvertip regarded him. For this was the man on whose brow the brand of Monterey was to be planted, the Cross and Snake.

The thing seemed hugely impossible. The man himself was a Titan; and around him were gathered the brutal ranks of the Drummons, those great-shouldered and heavy-jawed fighting men.

"You know the dog who put the mark on my door?" asked Drummon. "That mongrel called Silvertip? That fellow they say has the gray spots in his hair, just like horns?"

Tonio nodded. "I know him."

"What sort of a man is he?" asked Drummon.

"A man," said Tonio, "who is worth knowing. Most

112

things—they are nothing to him. He finds life very dull. The taste of it is like flat beer to him. But there is one thing that amuses him a little. That is to hunt a Drummon, and kill him; or to lead them like blind dogs across the country, and take the horses from six or seven of them, and send them home on foot. When he is ready, he'll come to the Drummon house and run them down as a cat runs mice."

Drummon stepped to the prisoner, swung his hand back, and struck him heavily, squarely, across the face.

The head of Tonio bounced back from the blow. A thin stream of blood broke from his nose and mouth, and descended across his chin.

Then the door opened, and the Runt came in.

He was like all the other Drummons in his main features, but he was qualified in two important ways. His bulk was condensed into a height a head shorter than most of his clan; and a frightful event in his youth had stripped the skin from his face, so that it was a silver white, streaked here and there with a grotesque patterning of red. All his features had been pulled slightly awry by the same accident, and the resultant draw of the skin. He walked with a distinct waddle and a sway of his broad shoulders, entering the room.

Coming straight up before the prisoner, the Runt said:

"There ain't more than one way to handle him. Fix him the way the Apaches fixed me. Take the skin off of him."

The whole clan applauded. And Silvertip would never forget the face of one man, the mouth gaping, the eyes closed with mirth, as he staggered this way and that, howling his glee.

"Who'll do the job?" asked the Runt, turning his head slowly, this way and that.

"Who but you?" answered Hank Drummon. "You oughta know how to work a skinning knife on human skin. The Indians done it on you, Runt. And this here is a pure Indian. He's just been gloryin' in it. Take a hold on him, and work slow, because I'm waitin' for him to break down —and you're the gent to do the trick."

The Runt, when he heard this, looked once more around the room, but this time with a frightful air of satisfaction.

He fastened his gaze, at last, on Tonio, drew out a knife, and commenced to whet the glistening edge of it on the sole of his boot.

All the while, he looked not at all at his work, but at the face of Tonio.

The Mexican was daunted, at last. That courage which had enabled him to endure the prospect of the torment, began to fail him when he saw the preparations in progress. For nothing in the world is so revolting to the man of Indian blood as is the thought of mutilation before his death. Christianity cannot dim the old legendary pictures of the unhappy warrior who goes broken and maimed to the happy hunting grounds, to perpetuate his shame and sorrows.

So Tonio looked at the bright flashing of the knife, and strained at his ropes, and leaned forward in his chair, in an agony of terror. No sound as yet had come from him, but he was white about the lips, and his nostrils flared with the beastly breath of fear.

The Drummons gathered close before him, shouting, laughing, pointing to his distorted face. And the Runt, having finished his preparations, took Tonio by the nose with the whole of his hand, and raised the blade for the first incision.

"Around the forehead first, right by the roots of the hair," said the Runt. "Then we'll peel it off in strips. I'll give him plenty of time to feel everything. Oh, I ain't goin' to hurry any more than the swine done when they worked on me."

He leaned closer over Tonio, and a shriek came tearing from the Mexican's throat.

Silvertip, with a groan, jerked up his revolver and fired. The chain that held up the lamp snapped in two under the impact of the bullet. The great double lamp fell, the flames leaping brilliantly up the chimney throats.

CHAPTER XIX

The Second Branding

THE round holders that supported the lamp were of strong iron, like the chain which had held up the heavy weight, but the body of the lamp itself was glass that shattered suddenly and completely. Flaming oil spurted to all sides; fire leaped in sparks, in crimson and yellow globules, in long streaks of brilliance, as high as the ceiling and far out to the walls. The whole room flared up with one might of illumination that died, suddenly, and left only dim welters of blue fire clinging here and there, spilling across the table, dripping in fits of flame to the floor, and on the floor itself giving out smudges of smoke, and rolling fire from whole pools of the liquid.

The chamber was filled with a mad dance. Shadowy bodies sprang here and there. One man hurled himself against the door, trusting to the impact of his body to cast it open, shattered. But the door held and flung him flat down in a pool of the flaming oil.

His shriek went upward shriller than the rest, as he rebounded to his feet.

Other hands tore open the shutters of the window. One,

and then another fugitive flung himself wildly out toward safety, and the first man began to roll on the ground like a dog, to rub out the fire that stung him.

Then Silvertip swung himself through the open window and ran forward. He had no knife. But that which the Runt had been prepared to wield was in plain view on the table. He snatched it up and made Tonio a free man with a stroke.

He heard the names of saints come grunting from the throat of the Mexican. The oil already had caught on the woodwork, and snakes of the fire were working up the walls and creeping along the floor.

They could not return by the window through which Silver had entered. Other men were fairly sure to be watching that exit. Tonio led the way toward the door that opened into the hall.

He swerved out into it with Silvertip running at his heels. Before him Silver saw the length of a narrow corridor. Women were in it, running forward, carrying buckets of water. Men came, also. Voices and footfalls thundered. There were hands brandished, and frantic faces of rage.

Silvertip fired three shots over the shoulder of Tonio as they ran forward.

He fired above the heads of the Drummons, because the women were there; because of the women, too, those shots were enough. Panic takes faster than fire in dead grass. The whole rout turned and poured back, yelling. Into doorways, down the next hall, they ran, while Silvertip and Tonio held straight forward toward the opposite end of the hall.

The window was open, there, and promised them escape. They dived through it as into water, tumbled on the ground, lurched to their feet again, and confronted a gun spitting fire, and a mighty voice that boomed through the night.

It was the voice of Hank Drummon, and Silvertip knew it. Something in the greasy huskiness of the sound was unlike the speaking of any other man. Tonio knew it, also, and as though convinced that no human power could avail against the power of this man, he threw up his arms in despair.

Silvertip, instead, was shooting.

116

He intended the bullet for the heart; he thought, when the silhouette toppled, that he had struck his mark; but then he saw the form struggle on the ground, and leaped at it.

He took Hank Drummon by the hair of the head, jammed it back against the ground and, in the dimness of the starlight, cut quickly, but surely. He felt the edge of the blade grate against bone.

"The second branding, Drummon!" he shouted, and sped away with Tonio into the dark.

There was no need for very great haste. Behind them, even the mighty voice of Drummon, shouting orders, could not bring order out of the chaos that had seized the household. Some of them ran here and there, probing a feeble distance into the darkness. But the majority, men and women, were laboring to extinguish the fire. Nothing, not even peril to human lives, seems as terrible and as important as the destruction which a fire works on a home. Bucket lines had been formed; both men and women, and children as well, were swaying the buckets forward, shouting to one another. The hiss of the water could be heard as it pulsed with a regular rhythm into the burning room. And huge clouds of steam and smoke, expressed through the windows.

From the shadows at the margin of the trees, the two watched the scene; and now and then a sudden flickering light within the house told that the flames were by no means conquered, as yet. Tonio, swaying from side to side, thumped his fists against his face and his breast.

"Now for ten good rifles, and we shoot them by the light of their own fire. Ah, Señor Silver! Now we could sweep them away!"

Silvertip said nothing. There was nausea in his heart and a tingling and shuddering up his arm; and still it seemed to him that he could feel the grating of the knife against the bone of Drummon's skull.

But he had accomplished the second part of Pedrillo's threefold task. One step remained. He might have made that, also, before aid came to Drummon in the dark of the night. He might have literally cut the brand of Monterey into the heart of his old enemy. But he could not have done that. He felt that he *never* could do it. He would have been glad enough if his bullet had struck the heart of Drummon; but he could not murder a man already wounded.

He brooded gloomily on that, as he stood beside Tonio watching the gradual subduing of the fire.

Then he said: "We'd better go back, because they're putting out the fire, Tonio, and they'll come straight for the Monterey house like so many hawks. It's war to the finish, now. Because the Cross and Snake is on the forehead of Hank Drummon."

They hurried back to the horses, mounted, and fled through the darkness, down the slope to the tarnished silver of the ford, with a few bright stars burning in the quiet waters of the margin. They put out those stars as they entered the stream. They came out on the farther bank and galloped, while Tonio shouted through the wind of the riding:

"Is it true, señor? Have you put the mark on Drummon?"

Silvertip waved his hand in acquiescence. He heard the Mexican break out into a wild, drunken song, swinging himself from side to side in the saddle with the rhythm of the music. It was a sort of laughing madman that accompanied Silver across the darkness and into the stern ravine which the house of Monterey overpeered, now, with a few lighted windows.

Only when Tonio came near to the house did he master himself, and as he dismounted in the entrance patio, he was as calm as ever. The same two vaqueros who had helped Silver depart, were now on hand to welcome him. But they gave him hardly a glance. Their gaping, their startled eyes, were all for Tonio. They insisted on touching him with their hands.

Then they heard the story of the brand that had been cut on the forehead of Drummon and seemed to go mad, as Tonio had been during the ride across the valley.

Some of them began to dance and yell on the spot. A few more reckless ones burst open the wine cellar and rolled out a keg which they staved in, ladling out great dripping portions to all who asked.

The sleeping children, wakened by the riot, began to run down into the patio. The domestics were already there.

The fierce, slender vaqueros poured in. Some one began to ring the great wide-mouthed bell which gave the signal of alarm and joy to the lands and the people of Monterey. Festival rang through the air; and in the midst of it, Silvertip saw the girl come out into the patio with Monterey.

She had on a black mantilla. She had on a black dress, too, with a red rose at her shoulder. As Silver watched her, he thought she was coming toward him—that she had singled him out, so that she could praise him for what he had done. But she paused, meeting him with her eyes only.

Monterey went to the first horse that stood near by, and swung up into the stirrup, standing there at ease in spite of the wincings and the prancing of the mustang which felt its withers wrung by the twisting weight.

He called out, and the crowd fell silent.

He was saying: "This is a good time for drunkenness and noise making! The brand is on Drummon now, and he'll be here soon. He has the law in his pocket. He can do as he pleases, unless the men of Monterey are wide awake. Tonio! Drive them out of the patio! Whip them out, if you have to. Get them back to watch posts. You fellows who have sworn you would die for me—you, Juan —you, José—Orthez—do you want the house knocked down about our ears? You knew there was reason to be on watch, to-day; there is a hundred times more reason now. A million times more!"

They obeyed him suddenly and cheerfully. Nothing could cool their spirits now. They were like an army which has been trembling on the verge of defeat, and which is now restored to a hope of victory.

Silvertip saw them scurry away, each to an appointed post, to take turn and turn about during the watch. For his own part, he felt that Mexican eyes and ears could be trusted more than his own.

They went into the big hall together, Monterey, and Silver, and the girl. They entered the library, where two lamps threw yellow pools on the floor without really penetrating the gloom. The girl had paused by the door.

"Come in, Julia," said Don Arturo.

"I am going to bed," she said.

"Going to bed before we hear from our friend the full story of what he has done?"

She kept drawing back a little as though she were afraid. There was something about her that made Silver want to go straight up to her and look into her face. But an odd constraint held him back.

"I don't think he'll talk about it," said Julia Monterey. "And I have to go to bed. I have a headache."

"Headache?" exclaimed Monterey. "Headache? Where's the Monterey blood in you? Now that you know the Drummon wears the mark—you talk of headache? Haven't you—"

He broke off suddenly, and then added: "Well, my dear, go along then, and good night."

"Good night," she said. "And Señor Silver, good night."

She went out; the door closed noiselessly behind her.

"What's the matter?" asked Silver. "There's something wrong with her. What is it?"

Monterey shrugged his shoulders. "What does it matter? I want to talk with you of the great thing you have done, my son. I want to know every step you made, and every gesture of your hand. Tonio is telling the peons his story, and the vaqueros are there, too, listening. Let me sit here and listen to you? Glory comes back to my house, and you have brought it!"

"I've told what happened," said Silver. "There's no more than that, and I'm no good at descriptions. But what's the matter with the Señorita Julia? Do you know?"

"She is afraid," said Monterey.

"Afraid? Of what?"

"Of you," said the old man.

The body of Silver jerked straight in his chair.

"You don't know why?" asked Monterey.

"I've no idea. What have I done to her?"

"Fair women, and brave men—that is the old story," said Monterey. "She has gone away for fear her eyes should tell you things that she would not speak with her lips. My friend, suppose that you seek her to-morrow, it would not be hard for you to learn what she knows."

Silver sat like a stone, staring.

Old Monterey stood up, moved to another chair, and sat again, leaning far forward.

"You have no real name—you hardly seem to have a

120

country. What is it that drives you around the world?" asked Monterey.

"A hard thing to name," answered Silver. "The hope of what lies around the corner. You understand?"

"A little. Tell me more."

"The other side of the mountain always seems to be best; the man I haven't met is the fellow I want for a friend; the town I haven't seen is the place I want to go to; and the house I'm not in is the one I want to live in. Does that give you an answer?"

"That gives me an answer," agreed Monterey, frowning. "And of women, also? I would not offer you Julia, except that she seems ready to offer herself. But now I can say that I am old, that the name of my family dies with me, and that your blood, señor, though it is not that of my race, would be nearer and dearer than that of any other man. If you marry Julia, you can be as a king on a throne, and in her there is nothing but courage, faith, and truth!"

He paused, and Silver fought to find an answer. He could live here, it seemed, a baronial life, freed from all care. The grandeur of old Monterey and the beauty of the girl moved him.

But suddenly he was saying: "You offer me everything that a man can give. But I can't take it. I can't change the fever in the blood, señor. I have to keep hunting; there always seems to be something waiting beyond the rim of the horizon."

"It's a foolish thought," said Monterey gently. "One person is about as good as another, and one place is about as good as another, also."

"I know that, too," said Silvertip. "That's common sense. But it doesn't keep me from chasing around the world hunting, and hunting. That's why I've left my name behind me. It would tie me down. I have a father and a mother, a brother and sisters. If I used my name, they'd locate me, before long. They'd look me up. It would tear my heart! They've looked me up before this, and I've gone back home and loved it for a week or a month. But then one day I wake up in the middle of the night, and the four walls of the room take hold of me like four hands, and hold me down. Then I know I have to go, and I go—before morning. I can't tell when the impulse will come. It simply grabs me—and then I've got to move on."

"No friends?"

"No close ones," said Silver.

"No family."

"I've lost it for good and all now."

"No home?"

"No, only a wish for all those things that keep me scampering. I'm a fool. I know that. But something has hold on me. I have to keep going on."

"Like the wandering Jew," said Monterey gravely.

"Well, I suppose there's something in what you say. Is there a curse on me, too?"

"You'll get over it," Monterey answered. "You think that you're condemned for life and as a matter of fact—Why, you're not thirty!"

"No," said Silvertip.

"Then you're simply being young—that's all. Good night! Go to your room and rest. The minute that there's so much as the stamp of a horse or the whistle of a bird, we'll call you. But we're all brave and strong now, because we have you with us."

Silver went to his room, closed the door and threw himself, dressed as he was, on the bed. The lamp still shone, but he was not troubled by that light in his eyes, as he began to think into his past and look blindly forward into his future.

He remembered what Monterey had said—that he was simply young—and it was like a promise of happiness and security to him. Under that influence he went suddenly to sleep. When he awakened, the rose of the day was pouring through the window, gunshots were sounding in the distance, and a hand beat furiously against his door.

CHAPTER XX

Bandini's Plan

THE gunshots no longer boomed distantly on the ear, by the time Silvertip had raced down to the patio. An outcry came from the watchers beyond the house; hoofbeats crackled over rocks or beat more dimly on the ground. And here came José Bandini with a small cavalcade, and a horse litter that bore a large, swathed burden.

Through the wide arch of the patio gate came José Bandini first, lean, erect, graceful in the saddle.

Utter loathing brought a faint smile to the lips of Silvertip. He turned his back on that new-come hero, and went into the house.

He did not see José Bandini again until just before the burial ceremony, when with all the other adherents of Monterey, Silvertip entered the chapel and filed past the body of the dead youth.

There was no alteration, it seemed to him, since he had last seen that face. It was still gray marble with a faint swarthy tinge of yellow in it, and about the eyes a shadow of blueness. There was the same sense of defeated weakness about the features; there was the same smile.

The hands were crossed on the breast. He touched them, and the thrill of mortal cold ran up through his fingers to his heart, as he recalled the vow he had made over the dead man.

Two parts of it were fulfilled. But before the third part was accomplished, all the mourners in this room might be dead.

He turned, and encountered the steady, strange glance of Julia Monterey, reading his mind as she had read it more than once before.

He saw José Bandini, watching him like a bright-eyed snake, and Arturo Monterey with head borne high and blank, dreadful eyes.

Afterward, they went down into the crypt beneath the chapel floor, where all the Montereys had been buried for generations. There they saw the coffin inserted in the wall, and the small door sealed over with cement. Even then, Arturo Monterey did not break down. And directly that they had come up to the patio, he called Silvertip and José Bandini to him. He took one of them on either arm, and walked up and down the patio with them.

"My friends," he said, "I know that there is bad blood between you. But this is the time to forget it. This is the last moment of my life, beginning. I know, with a very clear knowledge, that I shall not endure long. There is only one purpose remaining for which I can exist. You understand what that purpose is. I have made a vow, and you understand its nature."

He freed one of his hands, and touched the black band of cloth that encircled his forehead.

"Two parts have been accomplished," he went on. "You have done both things, Señor Silver, and it is a kind miracle of Heaven that lets you be still alive to walk here with me. But for the last of the three parts of my vow, no one man can suffice in action. It will need the strength and the wisdom and the courage of all of us. I don't know how I have deserved to have such friends gathered about me. But here you stand, and there is only one way for us to meet success. You must join your hands, my friends."

He took their right hands and tried to draw them to-gether.

José Bandini murmured: "Everything at your will, Señor Monterey."

But Silvertip shook his head.

He answered: "There are reasons that even you would not understand, Señor Monterey, why I cannot take the hand of Bandini. Let me walk aside with him, and I'll explain matters."

So he went off, with Bandini walking slowly at his side.

"*I* have no wish to take your hand, Silver," said Bandini. "I'd rather see the hand rotted off your arm by fire than take it in my own. Only, to please the old man—"

"You murdered Pedro Monterey," said Silvertip.

"You lie," said Bandini. His lean face wrinkled with a sneer. "Your gun killed poor Pedro," he said.

"My gun did the work, but you did the managing of it," said Silvertip. "How did he come to have your cloak?"

"We had been arguing a little," said Bandini, with de-testable smugness, "and I gave him the cloak, at the end of the argument, as a sign that we were reconciled friends again. That was all, in fact. A gift out of the kindness of my heart."

"Bandini," said Silvertip, "you knew that I'd look for you at that special hour that night. You were afraid. And you passed the cloak to young Pedro Monterey in the hope that I'd mistake him for you, during the night. And your idea worked out."

"You say this, Silver," answered Bandini, shrugging his shoulders. "But what you say means nothing. Every gringo is a natural liar."

"I am going to kill you, Bandini," said Silvertip gravely. "I warn you again. I'm going to kill you the moment that Monterey's work is done."

"Why do you wait?" asked Bandini. "Here is a time now. I am ready for you, Silver, night or day!"

Silvertip looked at him with curious eyes. "No," he answered, shaking his head. "You're not ready, José. You'll never be ready. There's a curdling of your heart when you think of having to stand up to me."

"D'you think so? Try me now, eye to eye!" exclaimed Bandini.

Silvertip smiled. "You know that I'm tied to my place here, with Monterey," he answered. "That makes you feel safe. But don't be a fool, Bandini. Sooner or later I'll have it out with you, and the sooner the better! Not here. Monterey wouldn't allow that. But one of these days, we'll meet outside the house."

"The minute you say," answered Bandini, "I'll be ready for you!"

They parted on that note.

Old Arturo Monterey moved calmly through the day. The sense of destiny about to be achieved never left him. There was in him a perfect surety that his vow would be accomplished, and Drummon delivered into his hands for the final vengeance to be taken. After that, he himself would die.

And he was ready for the end. Twenty-five years of brooding upon one purpose had perhaps unsettled his mind a little, and now the death of his son, the pinching out of the line of Monterey, left him ready to hurry to his grave after his great purpose had been accomplished.

For some time, there was no sign of danger from the Drummons. Perfect peace seemed to fill the bright days, and when scouting parties went out beyond the grazing grounds of the cattle, they rarely sighted so much as a herdsman attendant of Drummon.

No one was deceived. The danger was present, but merely delayed, and the Drummons were preparing their blow.

To Silvertip, it was a strange time. He had become, in the house of Monterey, a great figure. The Mexicans could not accept him as a friend; the age-long prejudice was too compelling for that. But they could look up to him as a force without which they could hardly win their war. So they attended him with respectful glances whenever he appeared, and he could not stir from the house without having two or three of the half wild vaqueros appear to join in his company of their own volition. Above all, Juan Perez was his shadow.

It was the second day after the burial of Pedrillo, that José Bandini encountered Silver in the patio and said to him, with a glance that moved grimly up and down his body: "Señor Silver, there is one great thing true in this world—that we hate one another. A gringo, like a swine, is able to lie in the mud of his passion; but I am not. I cannot sleep at night, Señor Silver, for thinking of the moment when you and I shall be face to face. And I have made a plan."

"Go on," said Silvertip.

"It's a simple one, and a good one. If the two of us fight near the house, the one who survives will be known as the killer. That is bad. When I have killed you, I lose my chance to get a reward out of the money box of the mad old man, Monterey. If you kill me, he will detest you, because he thinks that Pedro loved me. But suppose that we ride out, to-day, and come onto the lands of the Drummons—onto the verge of them. And suppose that we fight out our fight there, Silver? Why, then the one of us who remains alive can gallop back and talk about an ambush laid by the Drummons, and how *their* bullets killed the man!"

Silvertip scanned the face of Bandini with care. And then, suddenly, a fury of passionate hatred subdued all the soberer part of his mind and made him throw away suspicion.

"Bandini," he said, "get your horse, I'll saddle mine. And in two hours one of us will be finished!"

CHAPTER XXI

Tonio's Warning

OUT in the corral, the horses swept in waves, back and forth, as Silvertip advanced on them with his rope. He singled out the one he wanted, that same long, low-built bay which had carried him so well before, and dropped the rope on it at the first gesture.

Tonio came to him as he was saddling the broncho. There was concern in the big, round face, and the wise brow of the Mexican.

"You and Bandini, señor, you are riding out together?" he said.

"Yes," said Silvertip. "What's the matter?"

"He hates you so much that he groans when he hears your name," said Tonio.

"I know it," answered Silver.

"Hatred," said Tonio, "is a food that breeds thought. A great hate will make a fool wise. And Bandini is not a fool. I shall ride out with you."

"No," said Silver.

"Then keep eyes in the back of your head," went on Tonio. "I saw the face of Bandini, just now, and he was laughing to himself."

That warning from Tonio should have put Silvertip on guard, but the thought that he was about to confront Bandini face to face and so accomplish a great purpose, or end all things in the effort, worked like fire in his brain, and clouded and smoked over his better judgment.

He joined José Bandini, therefore, and they cantered side by side down the narrow ravine below the house of Monterey.

It was easy to believe that Bandini had been laughing before. He was still in the midst of a smiling humor, and when he turned his glance toward Silvertip, repeatedly there was a gleam in his eye and a chuckle from his throat.

"You gringos," he said to Silver, "think that you are the greatest fighting men in the world; and you, Silver, think that you are in the front rank of them. Now I'm not a distinguished man among my people, particularly, but—"

"No," said Silvertip. "Only distinguished for murder, not for fighting!"

"I am not particularly distinguished," went on Bandini, smoothly overriding the insulting interruption of his companion, "and yet, Señor Silver, this day I am going to eat your heart!"

"You're sure, Bandini," said Silvertip, "because you've learned a new trick in the pulling of a gun. Or you have a better revolver, and think that it'll act of its own accord. But that is only how you feel *before* we fight."

"Another lie!" said Bandini.

"No, it's true," said Silver. "The fact is that when you stand up to me, José, you'll turn into a snowman, and melt the strength out of your knees, and your hands will be shaking, and your heart will be beating in the hollow of your throat. How many times have you really stood up to a fighting man? You have a little reputation, but how many times have you earned it?"

He was amazed when José Bandini answered, with perfect cheerfulness:

"Never once! I've never had to. Most of the men I've met could be outmaneuvered. And any fellow's a fool if he thinks that it's dishonorable to take an enemy from behind. What does the lion do, for that matter?"

Bandini made a sweeping gesture to the sky.

"As the lion, so is Bandini," he said.

"And you're the rat that Monterey hired to teach his son how to fight?"

"If I'm a rat," said Bandini, who seemed willing to endure any epithet, "Pedro was only a mouse. He thought me a hero. I laughed continually behind his back."

They came out of the Monterey ravine, and thence rode across the valley of the Haverhill. Suddenly Bandini pointed out a group of low hills, though that was too large a name for them—they were mere swales of land, and over them grew entanglements of shrubbery.

"There's the place for us," he said to Silvertip. "When we get into that scrub, no one will be able to see us, and we can fight it out. Not an eye will fall on us, and afterward I can ride back to Monterey and tell him that unlucky Silvertip has been killed by sneaking, murdering assassins."

Silvertip said nothing. He merely smiled, and looked straight ahead as though already he were seeing a death—and not his own!

So, at the side of Bandini, he entered the brush and found himself in the midst of a small hollow around which the shrubbery gathered in what was almost a wall.

"Now!" cried Bandini, cheerfully, and sprang down from his horse. Silver followed that example, instantly.

"What'll you have?" demanded Silvertip. "Turn back to back and take ten steps? Or fire at the drop of a handkerchief? Take your choice—one way or the other—or anything else that pleases you better?"

"The first idea is a good idea," said the Mexican. "We turn back to back, and take ten steps."

"I take ten steps, and you turn at the fifth and shoot me through the back," said Silvertip. "That would be the way of it, and you know it, you yellow rat."

Again the insult slipped away from the easy mind of the Mexican.

"Well, then," he said, "you can tell me what next way you want. We can face each other—and the first man to go for his gun gives the signal?"

"Perfect!" said Silvertip.

He stood back a little. His shoulders dropped forward; his body flexed a trifle; a smile twitched at his lips, was gone, returned again; and his eyes shown.

"Are you ready, Bandini?" he demanded.

To his amazement, Bandini laughed loud and long, once more.

"Ready for what?" asked Bandini.

"Ready to stand your ground?" asked Silvertip, bewildered.

"But why should I stand my ground?" asked Bandini. "You fool, do you think that I brought you out here to put my life in your hands?"

And still he laughed, putting his hands on the red and yellow scarf that was bound about his slender hips, and swaying rhythmically from side to side.

Silvertip stared for one more moment. Then a shudder of apprehension went with electric suddenness up his spine. He turned his head, slowly, and saw, standing head and shoulders above the line of brush behind him, the grinning faces of four men—a Drummon every one. Two held at the ready double-barreled shotguns, one of them with sawed-off barrels. The others covered him with rifles.

And still the laughter of Bandini rang and beat against his ears.

In a dream, Silver turned his body toward the line of guns. He heard one of the men say:

"Take him from behind, Bandini. Rope him, boy!"

And the thin shadow of a falling noose flicked past Silvertip's eyes; the lariat drew taut, and he was jerked to his back.

CHAPTER XXII

Doomed!

THEY dragged Silvertip at the end of the lariat. Through the brush, they pulled him, while the thorns and the tips of the sharp branches ripped his clothes, and the flesh beneath them.

Then they paused to confer with Bandini, and let Silver get to his feet.

The conference was not long.

"Here's half your money," said one of the Drummons. "You get the rest from Hank, when you come to the house."

He was counting out greenbacks into the hand of Bandini.

"It's a pity to take the money," said Bandini, still chuckling. "I ought to pay you for this job. But now I have to ride back to the Monterey house like mad, and give the alarm: 'Silver is taken! The Drummons came down in force and mobbed him. I tried to help. But it was no good.' Here—put a few bullets in this!"

He pulled off his jacket and tossed it into the air. Three rifles cracked before he caught the garment again. Holding it up, he exhibited three holes that had been drilled through it by the volley.

"That is how bravely Bandini stayed and fought," said

132

the Mexican. "Monterey will thank me for that. There is only one trouble—that flat-faced Tonio loves the gringo so much that he'll be apt to suspect that I had a hand in his taking. However, we have to take these small chances. For I have to keep the confidence of Monterey, friends, if I'm to do the important work for you."

They spoke little more. Bandini merely lingered to say:

"Keep him alive until I get there. I want to see the finish of him. To-night, if I can, I'll go out by myself, like a hero"—he still was laughing—"and go all alone into that dangerous house of the Drummons—to rescue Silver, or die for him!"

The Drummons could appreciate a joke of this nature. They greeted it with a hoarse thundering of mirth. And as Bandini rode off, they started toward their own place, in triumph.

Like a band of wild Indians they galloped, dragging Silvertip on the ground behind them; and when they slowed enough to enable him to regain his feet, they were soon off again, jerking him flat.

His body was raw, his wits half senseless, by the time they reached the river. Through it they dragged him, and brought him senseless indeed to the farther bank.

When he recovered, they were working his arms and his legs to get his breathing started again. And he heard one say:

"If old Hank gets a dead man, out of this, instead of a gent that he can work on, he's goin' to skin us, and don't you forget it. Throw him up there on a horse, will you?"

They flung Silvertip into the saddle of the bay gelding which he had ridden from the house of Monterey. The lariat still bound his arms. His feet were tied into the stirrups. And gradually his mind cleared.

It was the end, he was sure. There was a sense of perfected doom that gathered over him. He had known in the beginning, he felt, that he would find his death in the Haverhill Valley. Julia Monterey had told him the same thing in clear words. He had guessed at defeat and at death when he was first in the village of Haverhill and endured the jests of the brutal clansmen.

Now they were gathered around him. His body was covered with a thousand cuts and bruises the sting of which set him on fire; and the warmth of his own blood covered him. His clothes were practically ripped from his body. He was a ragged statue, soaked in crimson, as they led him up the trail toward the Drummon house.

Their yells and the noise of their gunshots sounded far before them. A flight of hard riders came lurching down the way, men first, and then a scattering of half-naked boys riding bareback, all screeching like Indians.

They swarmed about the captive and the captors. They were like the creatures of a lost and barbaric age. One lad came near enough to plaster the blood of Silvertip over his hands; instantly all the others had to do the same. Here and there they galloped, yelling, waving their blood-stained hands, filling the air with their ecstasy.

And so Silvertip was brought over the brow of the hill and into sight of the house of Drummon.

The whole corner of it was blackened and charred by the fire which he had kindled. That in itself was a warning of what might happen to him at the hands of these savages.

He was dragged from the horse and hauled into the house to a room where Hank Drummon himself sat in a chair, with his wounded leg extended on another. Silvertip stood wavering before him, while Drummon ran his eyes little by little over the battered figure.

He was very angry, this chief of the clan.

"You done this for yourselves, eh?" said he. "You took and helped yourselves to him, did you? Why, you might 'a' knowed that it wouldn't be enough for me if there was twenty of him. I got that in me that could eat twenty like him! But you helped yourself to the cream, did you? You bring him in here half dead? Well, I'll see that you pay for it! Here—some of you throw him on the couch there, and some of the rest of you go and get cloth for bandages. Are you goin' to let the lifeblood all run out of him before I have my chance at him?"

It was done as he commanded, briefly and with rough-handed speed. They brought water to wash his wounds. Some thoughtful spirit had poured a cupful of salt into the dishpan, and the brine searched every crevice of the wounds with bitter fire. The sweat of agony rolled from Silvertip, as he endured, his jaws locked.

Then the wounded flesh was bandaged, and he was allowed the privilege of stretching out on the couch. His head rang still; and a hammer seemed to be tapping regularly at the base of his brain.

"Give him a shot of whisky," ordered Drummon. "I'm goin' to talk to this hombre. He oughta be worth talkin' to before he's bumped off. Hey, sheriff!"

For the front door had slammed, and now the grizzled, sodden face of the sheriff appeared in the doorway. He came in slowly, his eyes fixed on the swathed body of Silver.

"Here's the one that the greasers call Señor Silver," said Drummon. "Take a look at the murderin' hoss thief, sheriff, will you?"

The sheriff stood over Silver with his hands on his hips, and grinned and chuckled. "Kind of had an accident, brother, eh?" said he.

Silver looked up into the face of the man of the law, and said nothing. There was no help to be expected here, of course.

"I been lookin' into his record," said the sheriff. "It's a long one, Hank."

"What's he been and done, outside of the trouble he's made in the Haverhill?" asked Hank Drummon, and pressed his hand lightly against the white bandage that ran around his wounded forehead.

One of the younger men lifted the head of Silver and poured a glass of whisky down his throat.

He heard the sheriff saying: "He's one of these here self-defense boys. When trouble's in the air, he never makes the first move. He don't have to. One of them chain-lightning gun-trick boys. You pick your hand, and he fills it for you—with lead. One of them gents that are outside the law except on Sundays and holidays. One of them that keep movin', and move alone. That's the sort of a bird that you've caught here, Hank. How'd you get him?"

"Brains," said Hank Drummon, who never moved his eyes from the face of Silvertip. "Brains, and a little spot cash, and a dirty sneak of a traitor to deal with."

"You pry one of the greasers loose from Monterey?" asked the sheriff, astonished. "That's about the first time that was managed, ain't it?"

"The first time, but it ain't a Haverhill Mexican. It's that

135

slick greaser from the outside, that one called Bandini."

"I know him," said the sheriff. "I'd like to have the hangin' of him one of these days."

"Maybe you will," said Drummon. "But take 'em one at a time. I ain't through usin' Bandini. That lad's bright. He's goin' to show us the easy way into Monterey's house, I reckon, sheriff. And once we get inside that place, we're goin' to wash down the walls with blood! Understand?"

"I hear you talk, Hank," said the sheriff, "but you take an honest sheriff like me, and I can't listen to talk of killin' like that. It kind of rankles inside of me, to hear you talk like that, Hank!"

He roared with hearty laughter as he said this. Every one in the room joined in the pleasant jest.

And Silver, looking up at the ceiling, drew a slow, deep breath.

It was going to be hard, and very hard; but he kept his mind fixed far forward upon the future, when they would be bringing him toward the moment of his death.

He would have been sure of himself even if there were wild Indians to complete the tortures, he thought. But these devils were different. He could remember the Runt standing over the horrified face of Tonio; he could remember the frightful yell that had burst from the lips of the stolid Mexican at the mere thought of the thing that was about to be done to him. And how would he endure? He feared death far less than he feared the loss of his self-control.

"How many laid up?" asked the sheriff of Drummon.

"Five," said Drummon. "There's two of 'em down bad. The oil soaked into the clothes and kept the fire burnin' right into the skin, and down deep. And there's three more that's burned enough so's bein' up and around is pretty miserable. And there's me that's down, besides!"

He leaned forward a little and stared heavily at Silvertip.

"Yeah," said the sheriff. "He's done a job, all right. I dunno, Hank, but what we could make a *law* case out of this agin' him, except that you boys was about to skin Tonio, the greaser. That would kind of stand out agin' you in a court of law."

"To the devil with the law," said Hank Drummon. "The cursed Cross and Snake has been carved on *my* hide, sheriff. It's carved on there so deep that it ain't goin' to come off. And old Monterey is goin' mad with pleasure every time he thinks that two of the things he promised to me twenty years ago has been done. There's one more left to go!"

"Yeah," said the sheriff. "The door, the forehead, and the heart. I know!"

He looked suddenly over his shoulder, and his face puckered with horror and with disgust.

"I been shamed," said Hank Drummon slowly, the words bubbling huskily up out of his throat. "I been shamed and made a fool of, and every Drummon in the Haverhill has been shamed and made a fool of alongside of me. And it's been a swine of a white man that sides with greasers that's done it to me. When I start thinkin' about it, I pretty nigh lose the head off of my shoulders!"

"You'll keep your head on your shoulders," declared the sheriff, "until you've had your chance at workin' on him." He added: "What kind of ideas might you use, Hank?"

"I dunno," said Hank Drummon with a sigh.

He touched the bandage that made the round of his head, and sighed again.

"I dunno," he repeated. "Fact is, sheriff, that for twenty-four hours I been turnin' the thing around and around in my head. It might be that I could set by and see him stretched out on an ant heap. We got some red ants around here that sting like poison. They might start and work on him."

"Well," said the sheriff, "I always held to the idea that a gent sewed up in green rawhide, and left to be squeezed as the stuff started shrinkin' in the sun, would sure know he was dyin' for a long while before he finished off."

"It's an idea," agreed Hank Drummon almost tenderly. "I didn't think of that one, but I thought of other things, all right. I thought of leavin' him out where the blue-bottles would get at him. I wouldn't mind seein' him turned into a pile of fly-blowed meat."

The sheriff struck his hands together with a grunt of admiration. "You got ideas, Hank," he said. "You got a pile of ideas, and nobody can take that credit away from you! You got some of the best ideas that I ever heard about! Or hangin' a gent by the arms with a weight on the feet—that ain't a bad thing. The Indians, they used that idea often."

"They done that same thing," agreed Hank Drummon. "But I reckon that I'm goin' to improve on what the Indians done before I start to work on this gent."

"Yeah," agreed the sheriff, "suppose that you was to work on him and finish him off—you'd feel pretty sick if you thought of a better way afterward."

"I sure would feel pretty sick," said Hank Drummon. "He's put the mark on me. There won't be no way of takin' the scar off. When I get to hell, they'll take me for one of Monterey's beefs. They'll take me for one of the greaser's men when they see the sign on my face."

He groaned, and, closing his eyes, he allowed his great head to fall back against the edge of the chair.

"Whisky! Gimme a shot of whisky!" exclaimed Drummon, and held out his hand.

One of the younger men who had remained in the room, still feasting their eyes on the picture of the prisoner, instantly picked up a jug, filled a glass with pale moonshine, and offered it to Hank Drummon.

Hank tossed it off.

" 'Nother!" he ordered.

His cupbearer had seemed to know the drinking habits of the head of the clan, and the jug had been maintained in readiness. Another glass was filled, and the liquor poured down the throat of Hank.

"Now get out of here," said Hank Drummon. "The whole flock of you haul out of here and leave me be."

"Better have somebody around to fetch and carry for you, chief," said one.

"Get out and stay out! I'm goin' to be alone," said Drummon. "I'm goin' to lay here and look at this here skunk of a Silvertip. And I'm goin' to turn over ideas in my head. And it's goin' to be like listenin' to music to me to set here and think of what I'm goin' to do to him. It's goin' to be like a poet settin' and pullin' his hair, and waitin' for words, and lookin' at the sky, and admirin' of the birds. Get out of here, the whole tribe of you. Get out and stay out, and if I want anything, I'll beller at you fast enough. Just keep inside of call!"

CHAPTER XXIII

Bandini's Price

SILVERTIP lay in a spider's web. He kept thinking of that. The pain of his wounds, bathed as they had been in brine, did not cease, but grew steadily. Hammers beat in his brain; torment writhed in the pit of his stomach. He kept closing and unclosing his hands.

Conversation was forced on him now and then. For Hank Drummon, as he lay in his chair, brooding with eyes of insatiate evil, sometimes asked questions. He seemed to have an almost tender curiosity about the life and the character of this man whom he intended to destroy. And Silvertip told him stray bits about his adventures, about men he had known and fought with, about strange places he had visited.

Silvertip had no hope, and yet he felt that he was pushing the inevitable moment away from him little by little.

The evening came nearer. The strength which had run out of the body of Silvertip with his blood was diminished further by the long pressure of the pain. Here and there ragged rock edges had cut deeply into his flesh; but worst of all were the bruises which had hurt him to the bone.

Now and again a spell of dizziness nearly carried his senses away. And in every one of those moments he remembered suddenly the face of the dead man, Pedro Monterey, sallow, gray as stone, and smiling.

After all, the third part of Monterey's vow had been unfulfilled, and it would probably remain unfulfilled. The life of Pedrillo was lost; Silvertip, who had stepped into his shoes in the strangest of all manners, was about to die; and old Arturo Monterey would quickly follow them to destruction.

This brute of the fleshy forehead and the yellow-stained eyes had overthrown them all—he and the treachery of Bandini. Silvertip could forget even the pain of his wounds and his weakness when he considered how the consummate trickery of Bandini had twice succeeded.

It was dark, and the chief of the Drummon clan had not yet chosen definitely among the thousand schemes of torture which had been drifting through his mind.

Many a rare device had made him grin and smack his thick lips with laughter; but when he stared again at the big body of Silvertip and thought of what this man had accomplished already in the Haverhill Valley, besides uncounted exploits in other places, it always seemed to Drummon that his best ideas were inadequate.

Besides, there was no hurry.

There was no danger from the Montereys, for he had tied their right hand; he had paralyzed them by taking Silvertip.

Now he could sit back at his ease, like a spider that has lashed its victims in the sticky silk from its spinerets, and contemplate in advance the joy that would be his.

He was still contemplating when Bandini arrived, at the very moment when the supper gong was booming like a church bell, calling the Drummons to their food.

Silvertip, turning his head, saw the slender Mexican walk into the room, laughing, and, still laughing, come to stand over the prisoner.

"You see?" said Drummon to the traitor. "Silvertip's wearin' out. I been waitin' a good long part of the day for him to give up and start groanin', but he ain't quite weak enough yet. When we washed him in salt water, you could see the flash of his eyes as he rolled 'em from side to side.

140

But all he's been doin' since then is to open his hands and shut 'em, like a fish workin' its gills. He's in hell, Bandini."

"That's where he belongs," said the Mexican. "That's where he'll stay. But what do you mean by letting him stay alive this long?"

"What do I mean by—" began Drummon, his voice rousing to a roar of anger. Then he stopped himself and sat with his swollen face, puffing and glaring. "Well, Bandini," he said, "you've done your share of work for me, and you been useful. But don't start tellin' me what to do. I ain't used to it, and I won't stand it."

"You'd better stand more than that," said Bandini. "I can tell you things about this devil that you won't believe. I can tell you that where a snake can slip, he'll pass, also. I can tell you of pinches he's been in that would have cost the lives of twenty men, but he always gets out. The harder you shut your hand on him, the farther he pops away—like a wet watermelon seed."

"Yeah?" growled Drummon.

He swung his heavy head and glowered at the captive.

"Silver!" he commanded.

"Well?" said Silvertip.

"Your legs is free enough. Stand up," directed Drummon.

There was no point in opposing him. Silvertip swung his legs from the couch and put them on the floor. The move was an agony. He rose half to his feet, but there his bruised leg muscles refused to support him, and he pitched to the floor on his hands. His arms were strong enough, but the rest of his body was inert as a worm.

Both Drummon and the Mexican laughed loudly.

"You see?" said Drummon in triumph:

"I see," said Bandini. "It's all right if it's real, if he's not pretending."

"I'll answer for that," said Drummon. "If he wasn't made of whalebone and India rubber, every bone in his body would 'a' been busted by the dragging that they gave him on the way here. He's done for. He's as good as in a grave. All it needs is for me to pick out the right way of layin' on the finishin' touches."

"Lay them on soon," advised Bandini, shaking his head

141

and frowning. "His hands are still strong enough, and there's magic in them."

"You been useful to me," said Drummon; "but advice is something that I don't like and I don't want, no matter what you done for me."

"What I've done is nothing," said the Mexican. "What I'm *going* to do is the important thing."

"More important than catching that piece of wildfire?" asked Drummon, pointing to Silvertip.

The captive turned his head as he lay on the floor, and regarded Bandini. The Mexican stepped to him and kicked the prostrate, helpless body, not hard, but as a gesture of infinite contempt.

"Aye, Silver," he said. "I can do more than handle you. Brains, Silver; brains, Señor Silver. That's what a man needs to beat you. You have a fairly good head—but not strong enough in brains, Silvertip. And that's why I've picked you up in the hollow of my hand and closed the fingers on you one by one. You can listen to what my brains are working on now. Monterey—you came to fight for him. You'd take the place of his son. You'd be the hero, eh? Oh, you're a hero, well enough—but Bandini undoes all that you've tried to do—in one day!"

He turned back to Drummon, who was leaning forward in his chair, scowling with incredulity.

"I give you the Monterey house and all the people in it—at my own price! You understand?" said Bandini.

"Price?" shouted Drummon. "Price? I'll sell my soul and give you the price of that! Open the house of Monterey to me? Can you do that?"

"Aye," said Bandini, "and all that I want is part of the price of the things that are inside."

"Tell me what," said the other. "Speak out, you fool, before I burn up!"

"The price," said Bandini, "is all in one room. An old safe, Drummon. I want the lining of it!"

"You'll have it," said Drummon. He paused suddenly with a groan of distress.

"I know what you mean," he said. "It's the safe where the old man has piled up his money for twenty-five years. And you're to get that? It'll make you rich—it would make the whole Drummon tribe rich, too. But that's no matter.

142

What I want is to put an end to twenty-five years of waitin'. And the end may be comin' now! You mean what you say? You can open the house to us?"

"You give your word?" demanded Bandini.

"Give my word? Yes, and my hand with it! Here!"

Drummon stretched out his massive arm, but the other pushed it aside rudely.

"Call in the rest," he demanded. "I want witnesses. I want the crew of 'em to be witnesses."

Drummon's voice rose to the bellow of a bull; and all the pattering of feet and the noise of voices that had moved toward the house at the summons from the supper gong now focused like the sound of a storm toward the chief's room.

They came in a flood to answer him, the big, burly, heavy-faced men standing shoulder to shoulder, thronging around their wounded leader. And they stared hungrily down at Silvertip, stretched on the floor.

They seemed to think that the moment for ending him had surely come at last.

But Hank Drummon was shouting: "Here's Bandini wants witnesses that I swear to give him the safe of Monterey and every dollar that's in it, and I swear it now, in front of the whole of you. You hear me talk? Here's my right hand!" He raised it. "I'll give the safe to Bandini if he shows us the way into the Monterey house!"

"Into the house?" rumbled the chorus.

"Yes, into the house!" said Bandini. "There's an old door that leads to the cellar at the bottom of the cliff. It was walled up. But it's not walled up now, my friends. It's ready to be opened from the outside. I worked a few hours to-day, and the wall that used to block it up is gone."

They shouted. They smote each other on the shoulders. They looked about them with glimmering, drunken eyes. And the outcry which they had raised spread as if in strangely distorted echoes through the house, where women and children began to laugh and shout.

Presently Drummon cried: "We'll start now!"

"It's the best time," said Bandini. "They're weak as children over there at the Monterey house. They're expecting the sky to fall, and they're ready to run at a whisper since they've lost this Silvertip, this Señor Silvertip, as

143

they love to call him. Bah! The girl's white as a sheet, and shaking. Loves you, Silver, does she? Lost her heart to the great gringo, eh? Well, if you ever see her again, it will have to be in another world. Because you'll kill him before we start?"

He turned to Hank Drummon as he spoke the last words.

But Hank Drummon pursed out his lips and then shook his head.

"There ain't time to do the job right, and when this gent dies, he's goin' to die right."

He added, rolling from side to side in the chair: "Take me out of this. Rig that litter up. I'm goin' to be on hand when the Monterey house goes down. I'm goin' to be there. Here, Runt. You stay and take care of this gent—this Silvertip. Make sure of him."

"And leave me out of the big party?" shouted the Runt.

"Listen, Señor," said Bandini to the Runt. "To take care of Silvertip might be a harder job than to capture the Monterey house."

CHAPTER XXIV

The Time to Die

THE rage and the despair of Runt was a thing frightful to watch when he saw the rest of the Drummons throng out of the room. Hank Drummon himself could be heard cursing violently all the way to the outside of the house, where the horse litter was brought up for him, and the yelling of the Drummons went up through the brain of Silvertip like so many towering columns of flame.

It was the end of the Montereys, he knew. Suddenly he looked up to the ceiling of the room and wondered, desperately, how Heaven could permit him to lie there helpless while the Drummons rolled on, like so many wild beasts, to the accomplishment of their purpose.

The Runt stood over him with hands that moved and twisted like two great, hairy spiders.

"I ain't goin' to stay here!" said the Runt. "I won't be left out of the killin' of the Montereys! I'm goin' to get over there if I gotta wring your neck before I go—your damn neck!" he repeated through his teeth, and, leaning, he fixed his grasp on the throat of Silvertip.

The whole massive body of Silver was lifted lightly in the frightful grasp of the Runt.

But as the shoulders of Silvertip were heaved high, his long arms gave him the chance he wanted. Too late, the Runt felt the weight of the revolver slipped out of the holster on his thigh.

He released his hold, and Silvertip fell heavily back upon the floor. A shower of red sparks flashed in front of his eyes, but through them he was seeing the Runt and covering him carefully. And the Runt moaning, trembling with eagerness to attack, hung on tiptoe, controlled by the small, dark mouth of the gun.

"Pick me up," said Silvertip.

"You mean it?" asked the Runt.

"I mean it. Pick me up and carry me in your arms."

"I'll see you damned first," said the Drummon.

"D'you think I'll hesitate about shooting, Runt?" said Silvertip. "Pick me up, and handle me with care. You're strong enough for the job. Put me astraddle on your back, because I can't stand. And move slowly—my finger's on the trigger all the time."

Cursing through his teeth in long, whispering, frothing sounds, the Runt lifted that burden and shuddered under it. But the pressure of the muzzle of the gun against his body ruled him.

He opened the side door and carried Silvertip out into the open night.

There was little danger for the moment.

The men of the Drummons were, without exception, journeying through the night; slowly, because the horse litter that supported Hank Drummon could not be moved rapidly. And as for the women and children, they were gathered inside the big house, celebrating in anticipation of the ending of the long feud.

So the Runt got Silvertip safely to the barn. His back against the manger, Silver directed the choice of a horse and the saddling of it, and finally he was lifted up and his feet fitted into the stirrups, and then tied there, and the rope passed beneath the belly of the horse.

If there were a fall, he would be killed by the rolling of the horse; but there must be no fall.

At the door of the barn he gathered the reins and let the Runt step back.

"Don't follow me, Runt," he said. "It's no use. I'll be

safely off before you can have a nag saddled and get a gun. Run for your own life, because when Hank Drummon knows that you've let me get away, he'll flay you again the way you were flayed once before. But this time you won't live through it."

Then he loosed the reins, and the horse fled through the dark.

Every swing of that gallop was a torture to the rider. And his battered legs refused to take and sustain a hold, so that his weight kept slipping to one side and then to the other. With his hands on the pommel, he had to right himself, and the strength even of his arms began to give way.

He reached the river. Its bright face was a blurred flash, tarnished by the pain he endured.

The dashing of the water wet him to the shoulders, and was a blessing of assuaging coolness.

And then he went on, until faintness kept him gasping for breath. Twice he lurched far to the side, and the exquisite pain that he felt was all that rallied his senses.

But his head was bowed on the mane of the horse when, at last, he heard voices not far away, and looked up with amazement to find himself directly before the house of Monterey.

It seemed to him that there was a roaring of tumult in the air, and he thought that the battle must be in progress. But then he realized that it was only the pounding and the thundering of the blood in his own ears.

He came closer to lights. A voice shouted, and then many others joined in a chorus. Men walked beside him, supporting him. Others led his horse. He tried to stare through the bright mist and make out faces vainly. Then he heard the shrill, musical cry of Julia Monterey as the peons lifted him tenderly to the ground.

At that his brain cleared suddenly.

He could not stand. His whole body below the shoulders was limp.

"The outer door at the bottom of the cliff—the cellar door—Bandini has unwalled it from the inside to-day! D'you hear me, Julia? Bandini, and the whole crowd of the Drummons are down there, or almost there. Call the men and turn them loose. Start Tonio—where's Tonio? Where's Juan Perez?"

There was a rush of the party for the house, a storming of footfalls wending down into the cool dimness of the cellars.

He saw Arturo Monterey come for an instant into sight, then disappear into the house, calling orders loudly to his men. He saw Julia Monterey from a corner of his eye, he hardly knew where.

Those who supported him had dropped his body to rush after their master, Monterey. He lay sprawling. He raised himself to his hands and shouted out the name of the one man who, he felt, might come to him before all others.

"Juan Perez! Juan Perez!"

There was no answer.

It seemed to Silver that all the vast effort had been in vain, and that the oath he had breathed silently above the dead man in Cruces had been taken to no end, for now that the greatest need of Pedro Monterey's aid had come, his substitute had to sit sprawling on the pavement of the patio of the house, helpless.

"Juan Perez!" he screamed.

Then he looked up and saw Perez standing by him. Other feet were running close by. That was Julia Monterey. He looked at her face as through a fog. There was no need of women at a time like this. Men had died in this cause, and more men were about to die unless the premonition in his mind were very wrong indeed.

"Lift me, Perez—help me!" he said.

The strong hands of the Mexican raised him suddenly to his feet. Where the hands touched his wounded body, they burned him with fiery pain. But he was all one wound, and therefore the pain was not strange.

"I shall take you to a safe place," Perez was saying. "And I shall not leave you. Have no fear, señor!"

"Safe place?" groaned Silver. "Take me down into the cellars. Take me down into the old mine. I have a gun and I can still use it. Perez, lend me your strength and take me where I can help!"

"I shall!" cried Juan Perez. "Oh, that there should be such a man in the world!"

"Perez! He's dying now!" cried the voice of the girl. She tried to break in between them.

"Leave him—only help me take him to a bed," she commanded.

"Away with her—she's only a woman—there's no place for 'em now!" shouted Silver. "While we talk the fighting has started!"

"He shall have his way!" cried Perez to Julia Monterey.

"It will be murder, not fighting, if you go down among the guns!" she pleaded, turning to Silver.

"I tell you," said Silver in a frenzy, "this is the time to die!"

"It is the time to die!" echoed Perez, and began to help Silver strongly forward.

More help came to that wounded, half-naked body from the other side. He looked in bewilderment, and saw that it was Julia Monterey who had passed an arm around him and placed her strong shoulder beneath his. A good part of his weight she was supporting.

They passed through the door of the house. She it was who picked up a lantern, never relaxing her efforts to help sustain the half-benumbed body of Silver.

Juan Perez pulled open the tall door that led to the cellar. Out from the dimness came a medley of departing shouts that sank deeper and deeper into the gloom.

"Go back, Julia!" commanded Silver. "You're not needed. I don't want you! Go back!"

"No," she said. "Steady, Juan Perez! The steps are slippery."

"Julia, go back!" shouted Silver.

"It is the time to die," she answered. "Heaven knows how willingly I come to that time!"

"Perez!" cried Silver as he was taken swiftly down the first flight of the steps and into the gloom of a great gallery.

"Yes, señor," said Perez, already panting.

"Send the girl back! It is no place for her."

"Alas, señor," said Juan Perez, "she is a Monterey, and their women are as the men, ever ready for death."

Before them, out of what seemed an infinite distance, came explosions that struck with rapid impacts against the ear of Silver. And he knew that he was too late to be in the forefront of the battle. The men of Drummon already had come through the river door, and the shooting had commenced.

CHAPTER XXV

The Battle

As THE sound of the firing stopped their progress, with a silent assent, Silver said: "Julia, you know a place, perhaps, where they're apt to come if there's a retreat of Monterey's men. Is there one place they're apt to pass?"

"Two places, where big shafts join together," she said. "Ah!"

She cried out at a nearer echo of a death yell that rang out far away.

"Take me to one of the two places. No, tell Juan Perez how to go there, and then run back!"

"Turn to the right—here," said the girl. "Quickly, Juan Perez! There may not be time. The Drummons are so many devils, and our men cannot stop them. Quickly—quickly—if we are to reach the place in time where we may fight. Now to the left—now down these steps."

"Julia, tell us the way and go back!" shouted Silver.

"Am I a child?" she panted. "I shall not leave you. If you die, there is one of the Montereys ready to die with you. Juan Perez—faster—faster!"

150

They reached the bottom of a long descent, and then hurried forward to a place where several galleries converged in a meeting point powerfully sustained by great buttresses of the living rock. The lantern light glimmered brightly over the moisture that covered the stone.

"Now!" said the girl breathlessly. "If we place the lantern here in this gap—so!—the light shines down the passages they may come by. And we are left in shadow. Juan Perez, have you a second gun? I can shoot, also!"

They had placed Silver where he sat with his back against a wall, his legs sprawled out helplessly before him. With the lantern put in an adjoining corridor, it flung its light straight on down a mighty hall, where the pick marks showed on all sides, and left the three of them in the darker shadow.

"I have a second gun," said Juan Perez, "but that is for the señor. There is no way for you to help us now. Go back, señorita."

"Go back! Go back!" yelled Silver desperately. "There is no way that you can help here. Go back to the house—they are coming, Julia! Are you to stay here and drive us mad?"

"I am going," answered the girl quietly. "Juan Perez, guard him with your life!"

She was gone from the sight of Silver.

He heard Perez murmuring: "I have already sworn it. My life for yours, señor, and your life for mine. And that is the way that dying is easy. They are coming! Now we shall mow them down!"

"Look sharp!" answered Silver. "It may be that they are the men of Monterey retreating. Listen!"

For wild cries in Spanish now broke on their ears as the approaching tumult swept around an adjacent corner of the tunnels. And then the lantern light struck on a mob of frantic faces—the men of the house of Monterey in headlong flight, reaching out their hands before them as they dashed through the gloom, screeching out the names of their patron saints.

"Curse them!" groaned Juan Perez. "Oh, dogs who betray the hand that fed them. Look—the master is among them—he beats them—but they will not turn and fight!"

For yonder was the silver hair and the white beard of

Monterey as he was borne headlong by the current of the flight.

From the rear came the bawling voices of the Drummons in the height of their victory.

Now, behind the place where Silver sat, with a gun in either hand, and Juan Perez kneeling beside him in desperate readiness, he heard the shrill voice of Julia crying:

"Turn back! There is help here! Señor Silver is here—and Juan Perez—and great help! The fight is ours! Turn back, cowards! Turn back and face the bullets with me! Señor Silver is here, and he cannot die alone!"

He heard the girl's shouting as the leaders of the Drummon throng poured around the next bend of the hallway. He saw their faces gleaming white in the dull light of the lantern, like sickly creatures of the sea seen deep down in the shadowy water.

Right into the faces of those charging men Silver and Juan Perez poured a deadly fire.

He saw one man fall. He saw another pitch sidewise. He saw a third leap upward like a wounded deer, yelling. And the whole rout slowed, wavered.

A gap opened. In the rear he had a glimpse of the great form of Hank Drummon, borne on his litter by several pairs of hands. He had stripped himself to the waist, naked, like a sailor going into action on a battleship of the old days, and as though he expected to bathe in blood. In his hands were weapons. About his head was the broad white bandage. He seemed like a pirate picture out of the past.

"José Bandini!" he was thundering. "Show these cowardly fools the way to go forward. Charge the dogs! Charge 'em home and they'll vanish. Come on, boys!"

Into the van leaped the brilliant form of José Bandini. If he were a thousand times a villain, he was a thousand times a hero, also. He ran straight forward to lead the rest, and as he ran he laughed with the joy of the conflict, and waved a revolver above his head.

Behind him, the men of the Drummons rallied and surged ahead in a wave.

Silver, leveling his revolver, was about to fire with a deadly aim at Bandini when another form intervened before him.

It was old Arturo Monterey, running straight at his

152

enemy, with his white hair blown back from his head. He shouted a wordless battle cry as he ran.

The moment was lost to Silver. The next instant he saw vast forms bulking above him, and loosed the fire of his gun among them. Half lighted by the lantern, but only enough to make them jumping, swaying, whirling silhouettes, he saw the men of Drummon rush at him.

He saw the fine form of José Bandini lead the others. At that body he fired as Bandini leveled a gun and rushed at him, guided by the darting fires from the mouth of Silver's Colt.

It seemed a bitter shame to meet that moment seated. With a vast effort, Silver struggled to one knee. A bullet struck his body, he knew not where. The weight of the impact flattened him back against the wall.

A swinging foot kicked the gun from his left hand—that in the right was already empty. He was caught by the hair of the head and jerked forward on his face. And, turning as he fell, he saw Bandini lift a revolver by the barrel. That gun must have been empty, also, but a stroke with the butt of it would crack his skull.

His own hands were empty. But beside him lay Juan Perez, senseless, his face covered with blood that poured from a scalp wound, his arms outflung; and in the nearer hand, held out as though it were an offering in time of need to his friend, there was a Colt lying.

Silver threw up his left arm. The falling heel of the gun that Bandini wielded crushed the flesh against the bone, and beat the whole arm heavily down against his face.

But at the same instant his right hand had caught the weapon from the hand of poor Juan Perez.

"Take that!" cried Bandini. "I wish there were a thousand lives in you that I could beat out one by one. Gringo —take this! And—"

Silver fired upward, the muzzle of his gun inches from the body of Bandini. And the man fell forward on him, a loose, soft, warm weight.

The brain of Silver reeled.

He could hear two voices. The first was that of the girl, who was still crying out to the men of Monterey. And they had rallied. That was the meaning of the trampling and the stamping all around him. That was the meaning of the curses in Spanish and in English, one mixed with the other.

And the second voice was wailing not far away: "The Alligator's dead—save yourselves! Hank Drummon's dead!"

It was that yelling voice of dismay that beat the Drummons more than the sudden, fierce, and unexpected rally of the Mexicans. The cry that one man had started was taken up by others. As Silver worked the weight of the dead Bandini from his body and sat up, he saw the gallery filled with the thronging flight of the Drummons, the big men fighting to get one past the other. After them ran the victorious men of Monterey, yelling insanely with their victory.

Behind them were the dead.

It was amazing that so few had fallen in a fight so close and hot. Bandini was dead, to be sure. And two of the men of Monterey. And yonder sat the great Drummon in his litter, bloodstained about the breast where a great cross had been slashed with a knife, and under it a wavering line—the brand of the Cross and Snake!

On the floor beside him was a small body, with a head of white hair, but that body stirred, moved, stood up, staggering.

Juan Perez, who had recovered consciousness, was leaning over him, asking how he was. And then the girl slipped in between them and caught Silver in her arms, saying:

"Do you ask questions like a fool? He's shot through the body! He's dying! Call for help! If he's lost, there's no glory left in this day for the house of Monterey!"

CHAPTER XXVI

Geese Across the Moon

IF SILVER did not die, it would be because, said the two doctors who worked over him by day and by night, he obstinately refused to give up life, even when all that remained to him was only a little handful of the immortal fire.

But he lived, and when he could sit up in the bed, he learned the great tidings of events that had happened while he lay senseless, near to death.

The Drummons were gone. Their long fight, for generations, to win and hold the Haverhill Valley for themselves, had failed. Their leader was dead. Their spirits were broken. And they had sold out their lands for a song and left the Haverhill in a great procession of horses and wagons, like a picture of emigration out of an earlier day. Farther west and farther north, they would try to find a new home for themselves.

In the meantime, old Arturo Monterey, at the end of his life, had swept in for little cost all the lands that he had fought for so long. As for the village, it was gone. On the morning of the day when the Drummons moved out, a fire had started mysteriously, and in a few hours it was uncontrollably sweeping the place. Now rains were beating and winds blowing the black ash heaps of the spot where the place had stood.

All of these things Silver heard. And he could have guessed them, he often thought, merely by the sounds of song and laughter which, all day long, flowed through the house of Monterey—now near at hand, now sweet with distance.

He began to recover rapidly. The day came when he could walk, and then he could ride out with Juan Perez. And the peons in the fields ran to the fences and shouted and cheered him like a hero.

It made Silver laugh with joy to hear them.

Every day he rode out, and every day, when he returned, he felt that he was being brought nearer and nearer to the crucial point of his life. Monterey had said nothing; the girl had said nothing; but he knew that their eyes were waiting for him to speak. And the question that he must answer was as to whether or not he chose to spend his life here in Haverhill, now that it was purged of its plague.

If he spoke, he knew without vanity that the girl would marry him, and that old Monterey would leave the whole estate to her. But neither of them spoke, and he, day by day, tried to face the question, and could not.

His thought was totally in solution, and something from the outside was needed to precipitate it in the form of action.

It was turning cool now in the evenings, but still they dined on the garden terrace and in the twilight of this day a big golden moon came up out of the east and climbed softly up the sky.

A streak of shadow moved across it. Silver stared, and could not understand, for no cloud could be at once so narrow and so dark a line, nor could the wind blow any mist with such speed, he felt.

A breeze cut at them from the mountains. And Julia went into the house to get a heavier cloak. But old Monterey remained seated in his chair, his eyes rarely leaving the face of Silver.

It was the night when some word must be spoken, Silver felt. There was a warm and happy flow of temptation when he thought of the quiet days of contentment which could stretch before him if he married the girl and settled to life in the Haverhill.

And yet something checked him, and he could not tell what.

More often, day by day, he thought of young Pedro Monterey, to whom this place should have gone in right succession. He could think without sharp pain of the dead man now, for the vow he had made silently in Cruces had been discharged. And still Pedro Monterey remained the shadow on his mind.

So on this night, as he sat with old Monterey in the garden, he heard a vague sound come out of the upper air, and looked up, startled.

He could see nothing.

It was a cry that he had heard before, he could not tell where. His inactive brain would not place the note that had reached his ears. But it stirred infinite echoes within him.

"What is it, my son?" said the gentle voice of Don Arturo.

"Nothing," said Silver briefly.

But his heart began to throb uneasily. A melancholy desire for he knew not what possessed him.

He stood up and began to walk the terrace with rapid steps, feeling the glance of Monterey swing back and forth with him.

Again the dark, triangular line swept across the face of the moon, and a moment later the cry came out of the sky again.

Wild geese! Wild geese flying south! Now he knew what it was that stirred in his blood. He, also, wanted to be on the wing to another land. And suddenly the mountains on either side of the Haverhill rose for him like prison walls.

Again that half melodious, half brazen call came tingling out of the upper air and ran through all his blood.

"I'm going inside," he said thickly. "I'll get—something to put on!"

That was how he left them.

It was not many minutes afterward that Julia Monterey came down and looked eagerly, anxiously, but saw that Silver was gone. Monterey answered her look.

"He has gone inside to get a heavier coat," said the old

157

man. "He is very restless. He has been walking up and down the terrace. To-night, my dear, he is surely going to speak. And after that we shall be happy together forever."

"Restless? He may be restless to leave us!" she exclaimed. "What did he say when he went in?"

"Only that he was going to get something to put on. The wild geese had flown across the moon; when they called out of the sky, he looked up suddenly. And then I suppose that he felt the cold as he heard them, and he went inside."

"The wild geese?" she murmured.

And she in turn heard the distant chorus swept down from the chilly regions about. Between her and the moon the unseen hosts were flying and sending their harsh music toward the earth.

"The wild geese—and he has gone! He has gone to follow them. He has gone to—"

She fled suddenly from the terrace. Arturo Monterey stood up, startled and amazed. He cried after her.

But she, unheeding, ran on into the house, and hurried to the room of Silver. There was no answer to her knock. She threw the door open, and the darkness seemed to roll out just like a thick mist across her eyes.

She fled down to the patio.

"Señor Silver!" she cried to one of the house *mozos*. "Have you seen him?"

"Going toward the stable," said the servant.

"The stable!" moaned Julia Monterey, and ran on, breathless with fear.

It was near the stable that she met with Juan Perez, walking with his head thoughtfully bowed.

"Juan!" she cried. "Juan, have you seen Señor Silver? Has he been here?"

"Here and gone again," said Juan Perez. "There was trouble in his face. And he left this for you and the señor."

She snatched the letter and tore it open, to read:

MY DEAR FRIENDS: It came over me all at once, to-night, that I must go. I wanted to stay and say good-by to you, but I knew that you would be kind, and ask me why I should leave, and then I would be able to give no answer.

Forgive me for leaving like a thief in the night.

Some day I shall surely come to you again. From wherever I light, I shall write to you everything.

ADIOS, ADIOS.

She crushed the paper in her hand and ran across the patio to the great entrance arch, crying out his name. The sound of her voice passed down the road and echoed back to her emptily from the hillside.

It was dawn of the next day. High up in the center of the northern pass, Silvertip turned in the saddle and looked back on the blue of the river and the green, rolling lands that swept up from the stream. He could see the cattle as dull spots of color, and the distant house of Monterey was like a child's toy that one could have picked up between thumb and forefinger.

He looked at it until a certain mistiness came over his eyes. Then he turned and walked the horse little by little over the ridge.

He knew that he was leaving a glorious chance of happiness behind him; but he closed his eyes to it.

The chance was so great indeed that he felt it pulling at his heart with hands.

He would not surrender to it. The old unrest moved in him like new blood. The wind of the mountains vainly caused his new wounds to ache.

He set his teeth firmly and aimed his course toward the blue and crystal-white of distant mountains.

SONS OF TEXAS

Book one in the exciting new saga of America's Lone Star state!

TOM EARLY

Texas, 1816. A golden land of opportunity for anyone who dared to stake a claim in its destiny...and its dangers...

___SONS OF TEXAS   0-425-11474-0/$3.95

**Look for each
new book in the series!**

Check book(s). Fill out coupon. Send to:

BERKLEY PUBLISHING GROUP
390 Murray Hill Pkwy., Dept. B
East Rutherford, NJ 07073

NAME_____

ADDRESS_____

CITY_____

STATE_____ZIP_____

**PLEASE ALLOW 6 WEEKS FOR DELIVERY.
PRICES ARE SUBJECT TO CHANGE
WITHOUT NOTICE.**

POSTAGE AND HANDLING:
$1.00 for one book, 25¢ for each additional. Do not exceed $3.50.

BOOK TOTAL $ ____

POSTAGE & HANDLING $ ____

APPLICABLE SALES TAX $ ____
(CA, NJ, NY, PA)

TOTAL AMOUNT DUE $ ____

PAYABLE IN US FUNDS.
(No cash orders accepted.)

203